I0638835

DARK CROWN

Guardians of the Fae Realms: Book 8
JL Madore

Copyright © 2021

All rights reserved. No part of this publication may be reproduced, distributed or transmitted in any form or by any means, without prior written permission.

JL Madore

Cover Design: Ravenborn Covers

Note: The moral right of the author has been asserted.

This is a work of fiction. Names, characters, places and incidents either are the product of the author's imagination or are used fictitiously, and any resemblance to actual persons, living or dead, business establishments, events, or locales is entirely coincidental.

No part of this publication may be reproduced, stored in a retrieval system or transmitted, in any form or by any means without the prior written permission of the author, nor be otherwise circulated in any form of binding or cover other than that in which it is published and without a similar condition being imposed on the subsequent buyer.

The scanning, uploading, and distribution of this book via the Internet or via any other means without the permission of the author is illegal and punishable by law. Please purchase only authorized electronic editions, and do not participate in or encourage electronic piracy of copyrighted materials.

Your support of the author's rights is appreciated.

Dark Crown: Guardians of the Fae Realms

JL Madore -- 1st ed.

ISBN: 978-1-998372-65-2

AUTHOR NOTE

Hey, Hotties:

Dark Crown is book three in Nakeyla Northwood's harem trilogy and book 8 in the Guardians of the Fae Realms series.

If you missed the first harem and the intro to how we got here, start at book 1 of the entire series as this story is a continuation of plot and cast of character from the first group of lovers. Guardians of the Phoenix.

If you've read that and loved it all, the first book of Honor's harem Honor Restored is up for preorder to continue after this. Here's a teaser for you... you've already met at least two of her guys. Can you guess who they are?

JL

CHAPTER ONE

Keyla

S tanding on the dais of the throne room in Thornebane Castle, my mates, my family, and I look out upon the anxious faces of traitors, cowards, and the tormented. The opulence of the space, packed with close to three hundred fae citizens, is everything I'm accustomed to having grown up a princess of another realm.

The people packing the room are not.

The sea of bodies is as different in size, shape, color, and species as they could be. In the Human Realm, the fae community consists of those who naturally pass as human or those who have the magical ability to glamor themselves to remain unseen.

The population of the Fae Realm is everyone that excludes… gnomes, nymphs, forest folk, dragons, etc.

"I'm sure, many of you are wondering why I've called you all together," Creed says, his deep voice projected to reach the ears at the back of the room. "Some of you have surely heard rumors. Others might know firsthand, but I am pleased to announce that three days ago, in a battle fought in the Travon badlands, Laryssa the usurper of our quadrant was put down and eliminated from this life."

There's a rush of murmuring through the crowd and Creed gives them a moment to settle. "I won't apologize for her death, in fact, I celebrate it. Over the past two years, she has held my sister hostage and bound me to submission with the threat of killing Princess Honor and my mother should I resist."

Watching the crowd, I'm happy to see so many horrified looks flashing around the room. Most of them weren't aware of the depths of Laryssa's treachery.

"I learned only days ago that the threats against my mother were hollow. Our beloved Queen Thornebane perished the night of the rebellion and progressed to the Sacred Grove alongside my father."

An outpouring of sadness and sympathy fills the air.

"However, with the help of my new mates and the Phoenix Quint, I am relieved to inform you Princess Honor was recovered and Laryssa's leverage over me ceased to hold power. My bride and her family helped rescue my sister and end Laryssa's madness. Dornte is once again under the rightful rule of the Thornebanes."

There is an uproar of cheering.

The majority of his people look relieved and excited, but some definitely don't.

"To those who acted against me, be warned. Over the next few days and weeks, I will interview each one of you personally. As a powerful Mind Guardian, I will weed out those loyal to Laryssa, those of you who plotted in the initial uprising against my family, and those of you who don't celebrate my return to power. If you fall under any of those categories, this is your only warning—get the fuck out of my castle."

No one moves, but I smell the acrid burn of fear rising in the air. It offends my wolf. I growl and let her ascend until my eyes glow gold.

"I offer you this warning as a kindness not given to my parents. Consider yourself lucky to leave with your life. Get out of my home and my quadrant. Do it quickly or you will join the bitch queen you favored."

My wolf surges forward, howling inwardly in support of my mate's unyielding stance.

"For everyone else, know this... I understand how Laryssa manipulated, threatened, and forced her will upon innocents. I was not the only victim of her malicious ways. For you, I extend my understanding and forgiveness. Stay. We will heal these wounds together."

"Blessed be, King Creed," someone yells from the back. The room breaks out in the echoes of support and well-wishes.

After a moment, Creed lifts his hands to quiet the crowd. "I appreciate your encouragement, I truly do, but it's too early to celebrate. We have cut the head off the snake holding us in her coils but a great many wealthy, ambitious, and corrupt people supported Laryssa. They won't appreciate me returning the power of choice and freedom to the citizens of Dornte. Be hopeful but remain vigilant. There are still battles to be fought."

I slide my arm around his hip and hug tight to his side and then I gesture to Dillan and Rhylan at our sides and Kotah and his mates at our backs. "But those battles won't be fought alone. Rest assured, the magic of fae destiny bonded us together for a purpose. We honor and embrace our place supporting your realm."

"It's your realm too now, my queen," Creed smiles down at me and the love and relief in his obsidian eyes make my wolf howl.

"Kiss her, King," someone yells.

He grins at me. "Do you mind?"

I chuckle. "Mind you kissing me or being ogled by three hundred people while you do it?"

"Either."

I reach up on my toes and tilt my head back. Creed has an aggressive, alpha way about him that steals my breath and dampens my panties. He wraps his arms around me and claims my mouth.

There's no hesitation about the propriety of this being a public display. He kisses me here as he kisses me behind closed doors—with passion.

The moment our lips touch and I smell his desire, my wolf and I are lost to the primal pull of our searing. The fae universe paired our souls as a perfect match of perfect mates.

We complete one another.

We complement one another.

I'm entirely consumed by his tongue in my mouth and my nipples peaking beneath my blouse. Gone is any thought of decorum until Doc's amusement flashes onto my mental radar and I realize we're still standing in front of his staff and subjects.

Reining it in, I nip his lip and tug at it as I ease back. Opening up a private telepathic channel, I speak straight into his mind. *Sorry about that.*

Not your fault. He straightens and scrubs a hand over his mouth. When he looks out at the room full of people, he chuckles. "You came for an announcement and got a show. Apologies, we haven't been mated long enough to navigate the pull of our soul-searing yet."

"You're the king," Rhylan says at Creed's left. "You don't need to apologize."

"Especially for loving your young bride," a woman halfway back in the room says. "It's lovely, Prince—I mean, King Creed."

Creed chuckles. "I guess there are things we all have to get used to over the next weeks."

I squeeze his hands and catch my breath. "Don't forget about the suggestions."

"Right. Thanks, angel." He looks out at his people and smiles. "Since I was bound to the sidelines for over two years, Keyla and I worry we might be out of touch with everything Laryssa did and inflicted on the quadrant. When you come to see me for your interview, there will be a datapad available for complaints, comments, questions, and concerns. Feel free to submit a note of anything you want us to consider or be aware of."

I see the arched brows and smell the trepidation in the air. "We'll set it up to be anonymous but if you wish to address something directly, you can add your personal information into the notes and we're happy to speak to you as well. We will rebuild what she took from you. We're dedicated to restoring the Thornebane reign."

When everyone falls silent, Rhy leans forward and smiles. "Is everyone finished?"

Creed checks with me and I shrug and nod.

"I think that's it for tonight," he says.

"All right, everyone," Rhylan says, addressing the crowd. "Thank you for coming. For those of us looking forward to the reign of a true leader, it's an exciting time. For those of you loyal to Laryssa, your window to leave the castle peacefully is closing. Gather your things quickly, get out, and be thankful King Creed is cut from a different cloth than the usurper bitch that held us prisoner for the past two years."

I keep my expression blank. Not the way I would've finished the evening, but hey, Rhy was tormented too.

Besides, the people seem to agree with him.

The doors at the back of the room open and people begin to file out. The buzz of excitement in the air and the energy of the room are largely positive.

A couple of dozen citizens make their way up to the dais and either bid us their best wishes or bow or gush over the Phoenix and her Guardians.

Twenty minutes later, we're walking back through the castle toward the royal heirs' suite.

Thornbane Castle is fascinating and inspiring.

Like the palace where I was raised, it's partly a royal residence and partly a governmental and military base of operations. It's the hub of the ruling order for this quadrant and it has the old-world charm of an ancient Scottish castle.

Filled with interesting nooks and alcoves, I take in the long tapestries hanging in front of the hidden pockets of rooms. What lies behind is often obscured from view.

I lean and tilt my head to discover what mysteries they hold. Some have paintings or sculptures, and some have leaded windows with spectacular views of the Dornte quadrant.

In the weeks to come, I look forward to exploring each one at length.

In high spirits, our group of nine rounds the corner toward the private residences of the royal family.

Rhylan says goodnight and falls back, retreating to his guard's quarters. I don't like the distance he's keeping from us, but suppose he's dealing with a lot and needs some time to himself to process.

As we close in on our suite, I turn to Kotah and his mates. "Are you guys coming over for drinks or retiring for the night?"

My brother shifts his gaze to Calli to give her the choice to make.

"I'd like to say goodnight to Rile—Honor and then turn in," Calli says, meeting the gazes of her mates. "Are you guys good with that?"

Kotah nods. "Of course, *Chigua*. I'll sit with you if you don't mind the company. Perhaps I might ease Honor a little."

Jaxx grins and winks at his female. "We'll wait in our suite, kitten. Take your time."

Creed presses his hand on the security scanner next to the door and unlocks things. Normally he doesn't keep the suite locked when there's someone inside but with Honor defenseless, he's taking every precaution.

What he said during his address to his staff is correct. There are a great many wealthy and influential people who won't be pleased about him assuming his place as king.

Creed escorts Calli and Kotah inside to check on Honor and it strikes me that now is as good a time as any to speak to Hawk.

When Doc holds the door for me, I shake my head and point to Hawk. He understands immediately and continues inside to close the door.

Brant, Jaxx, and Hawk don't notice my intention and head across the corridor. Before they go inside, I catch their attention. "Would you mind…" I lower my voice. Kotah might be inside my suite with the door closed, but our heightened sense of hearing doesn't mean he won't hear me. "Could I speak with you guys for a sec, privately?"

Hawk frowns and tilts his head toward their suite. "Of course. Come into our office."

Creed

When Keyla remains in the corridor, I understand why immediately, and I do my part to not raise Kotah's curiosity. Escorting him and Calli through the suite, I pause at the door to Honor's bedroom. "Thank you all for standing with me through the past week and helping us reclaim the quadrant. I am forever in your debt."

Kotah rests his hand on my shoulder, and I'm immediately washed with the rush of serenity that comes from him being an omega. The Wolf King is a wonder to me on several fronts. He isn't even twenty-one yet, but he possesses deep-seated wisdom and maturity that goes well beyond the year on his birth certificate.

Bearing the same graceful build, long, chestnut hair, and wine tattoo banding his throat as his sister, Kotah and Keyla are unmistakable as siblings. "You are forever welcome, my brother. Make her happy and be the leader your people need. That will be thanks enough."

"And you are well on your way to both those things, by the way," Calli says winking. "You guys crushed it with the announcement tonight and the sexy schmexy between you and Keyla brought a lot of smiles to the room. Your people are hopeful for a kind and caring leader and our girl is practically walking on air."

Good. I thought as much but it's nice to hear it... especially from Keyla's closest girlfriend. "She's easy to love. I can't tell you how blessed I feel."

Kotah wraps his arm around Calli's shoulder and brushes the back of his fingers down her cheek. "You don't have to tell us. We understand completely."

"I suppose, of anyone, you do."

Calli rolls her emerald green eyes and tilts her head toward the door to Honor's suite. "Let me check on my BFF before this love-in gets too mushy. Then we'll all turn in for the night and the blessings of fated mates can get underway."

Kotah grins. "Sounds good to me."

The three of us enter Honor's bedroom and Lukas stands from the cushioned bench by the window. More than the military man he appears, Hawk's right-hand man is also a powerful mage and a dedicated member of Keyla's extended family. "How did the address to the castle go?"

"Very well," Calli says. "Creed's family are obviously loved and respected as the rightful leaders of this quadrant. Almost everyone seemed pro-Thornebane."

"That's good. Congratulations."

I nod and accept his well-wishes.

"How's my girl?" Calli asks, rounding the bed to sit with her.

Lukas glances down to where my sister lays unconscious. "I attempted to unravel some of the witch's hold on her, but the spell is complex. I won't give up, but I'm not sure anything I do will help."

"I'm sure it's helping," Kotah says. "Your efforts are always effective and you're far too modest."

Lukas doesn't look so sure, but I tend to agree with my brother-in-law. After standing with Lukas in battle and watching him take on the witch and foil every strike she made against us, I have faith we'll get Honor back.

"Thank you for sitting with her. I believe the worst of Laryssa's hold was severed with her death, but I'm not willing to bet on that with my sister's safety."

Lukas dips his chin. "Understood. It's my pleasure to sit with her. She's a strong woman and has suffered enough. She deserves the respite."

She does.

Calli sits at the bedside chatting with her and honestly, I can't imagine the two of them as best friends. Sure, they're both strong and feisty women, but Honor has always been serious and driven. She can be hard-headed and domineering.

Calli is the opposite.

Maybe that's it.

Maybe they are each other's complements.

Rounding the large paneled bed opposite Calli and Kotah, I sit on the edge of the mattress and gather her hand in mine. I revisit my thoughts of a moment ago of the similarities between Keyla and Kotah.

The same can be said about Honor and me.

The two of us are both tall, strongly muscled, and wear our white hair long—hers to the small of her back, mine to my shoulder blades. Our wings were always the same too—turquoise and black with a rare iridescence I thought regal—until Laryssa had me butchered.

The loss of my wings is a devastating reminder of that hateful woman.

One I'll never be rid of.

When Doc first examined Honor three days ago after her rescue, I feared she might have suffered the same brutality. It's difficult to tell as mind guardians retract our wings when we don't need them. Thankfully, her wings seem to remain intact.

Her back is smooth and clear of any scarring.

Unlike mine.

I'm not so naïve to believe she doesn't bear other scars. I was there when Laryssa had her brutalized by the guards. I have no idea what other kinds of horrors she suffered while under Laryssa's control.

I don't even want to imagine.

"Okay, so that's the update," Calli says, patting her arm. "You can be really proud of your big brother. He set the quadrant straight and set the framework for the Thornebanes to kick ass and take names." She looks over at me and winks before straightening. "Now, I gotta bounce and spend some time with my guys. I'm across the hall if you need me, girlfriend. Keep healing and working your way back to us. Lurve you."

When I rise to walk them out, Calli gives me a playful smack to my abs. "Don't look so worried. She's in there and she's fighting her way back to us. I have no doubt her eyes will open soon."

I force a smile and try to believe that. "From your lips to the ears of the gods."

Rhylan

While Creed, Keyla, and Doc deal with family drama, I retreat to my suite, grab a couple of bottles of ale out of my fridge, and let the new normal sink in. We've only been back in the quadrant a few hours. We took the time to shower, change, and ready for Creed's address.

Now that the whirlwind of the past week and a half is slowing down, the reality of my life is setting in. I chose Creed over my family and Vikarus will never forgive me. I'm a traitor in the eyes of my dragon brood. And I've likely condemned my family name to be erased from the ancient scrolls in disgrace.

Wow. I accomplished a lot in one week.

The only good to come out of any of it—I'm not alone in the fallout of my life.

I'm mated to Creed now—and by extension, Keyla and Doc. They've got my back even though Vikarus wants nothing to do with me.

"My brother... my real brother would know that nothing is more important than our family honor."

But what is a man's honor worth if he sacrifices his soul to save face and please the wrong people? Doesn't it preserve my honor to make the hard choice and commit to what's right no matter what the cost?

I set the bottles of ale on my table and sit to unlace my combat boots. When those are off, I unbutton my shirt, pull it off, and hang it over the back of my chair.

Pssst. The hiss of the seal breaking as I open the first bottle is a balm to what hurts. I'll hear that sound a lot tonight because I intend to get obliterated and pass out unconscious on my bed.

It may have been three days since the raid at the compound but between getting Honor back to Travon, finding a clinic, and waiting for a med-tech to clear her for portal travel, there wasn't time to evaluate what life would be like when we got home.

I tip my head back, get my throat moving, and guzzle the first bottle to start this ride off hard and fast. A knock behind me brings my attention to the open door of my suite and I lift my chin to greet Dillan. He's the other plus-one mate in this messed-up marriage.

"You need something, Bear?"

Stocky, muscled, and educated, he's one hell of a solid guy. He's hot too. He's got the same dark black hair as his bear's pelt, is a scrappy fighter, and one hell of a soldier.

There are some things only men who serve in a military capacity can understand.

I get the feeling Doc gets me more than most.

I hand him one of the chilled bottles and go back to grab a few more. "Yes, I'm avoiding the foursome. Yes, I'm brooding and wallowing in my misery. Have you been sent to bring me in?"

Doc holds up his hands in surrender. "Nothing like that. Everyone is busy doing their thing, and I thought I'd check-in and make sure you're okay. Being back here now that everything has changed can't be easy."

No. It's not.

I twist off the cap of my next bottle and take a long gulp. "I don't know why I thought he'd understand. Vik has a thick skull and a code of conduct that demands things remain either black or white. There is no coloring outside of the lines or veering from the mission for him. All he sees is me betraying my station and dishonoring our family."

"It's early days. Trust me. When it comes to stubborn hotheads, Vik's got nothing on the bears in my family. He'll come around once he gets over the shock."

I don't think so, but it's nice to hear.

Doc opens his beer and tosses the lid onto the table with the others. I watch his throat bob as he guzzles down the liquid inebriation and breathe a little deeper.

Before this mess, this is exactly the kind of night I'd sneak across the corridor and obliterate my reality with a few hours of punishing sex with Creed.

That man is a machine.

Now that's not an option.

Maybe I'm hyper-focused on Vik so I don't have to think about the mating stuff. I chug back a few more gulps. I don't want to think about the mating stuff.

It's a tough situation all around.

"I guess we've got some awkward conversations ahead of us. What do we do? Take turns? Have designated nights? Draw names?"

Doc chuckles. "Been there. I said almost exactly the same thing to Keyla last week. The three of us have pretty much worked through the worst of things now. Drinking helped at first, but time spent together helped more. We'll get there. There's no rush."

I set down empty number two and crack open the next bottle. The buzz of my mental tailspin is slowing a little in my mind. Another couple of bottles and I should be able to sit still long enough to relax. "I'm honestly not interested in getting into it tonight. I'm bagged and in no mood to jostle sleeping arrangements. Four in a marriage... it's more than a bit messed up."

"Nah. It's fine," the bear says. "There's no 'have to' with this. You had the shit kicked out of you over the past week. Don't force it. Just know we're here when you're ready to talk it out or lose yourself in some warm and wet or even if you want to fuck away some hostility. The bed might be crowded, but we'll manage."

"Honestly, a couple of those options sound pretty slecking good right about now. Except, I'm in a shit mood. No offense, but I think for tonight I'd rather drink, wallow, and black out."

Dillan raises his bottle and clinks mine. "Understood. Enjoy your solitude. Just remember if you need us, we're across the hall. You don't need an invitation. You belong in there with us. We *are* your mates."

That will take some time to wrap my head around. "Thanks, Bear. I appreciate it. And don't worry. I'll sort my shit out and get my head in the game... just not tonight."

Dillan raises his bottle in a toast. "Fair enough. Just know we'll be naked and down and dirty the moment we're settled in. If you change your mind and want to lose yourself, join us. It's always a good time."

CHAPTER TWO

Doc

*L*eaving Rhylan to his thoughts, I head back across the hall and into Creed's suite. Huh, I suppose I should start thinking of it as our suite. Rhylan's not all wrong. The way the four of us ended up mated is a little messed up and takes some getting used to. Still...

This is us.

With Keyla across the hall in the quint's suite talking to Hawk, Brant, and Jaxx, and Creed in with Calli, Kotah, and Lukas checking on Honor, I'm left to a rare moment of finding myself on my own.

Growing up in a big family of foster brothers and sisters, and then enlisting and serving overseas, I'm accustomed to a lot of people around most of the time.

I'm good with that.

Truth be told, I prefer quiet time—one-on-one.

Or maybe in this case two on one.

Or three on one.

Images flare in my mind and my cock stirs in my jeans. I've

witnessed some of the sexual hijinks Brant and the quint get into. I understand why Keyla wants that. I don't blame her. Now that I've opened myself up to the possibility—I do too.

I never imagined myself in a polyamorous marriage. Growing up, I had my future mapped out: great girl, a house on a little patch of land, and eventually a bunch of cubs to raise. Perfect, right?

Now I'm in a foreign realm with three mates.

I still ended up with a great girl—though it's a castle in a large quadrant of land. And she's much too young to start thinking about cubs. Now that I am thinking of it, maybe they won't be cubs.

Creed mentioned that the first two kids in his lineage are always a boy then a girl to stand as heirs to the Dornte throne. And after the mind fae children? Will the rest be bears or dragons or wolf pups? Does it matter?

Talk about a mixed marriage.

It's different for the quint. As the mythical phoenix, Calli can only conceive if all five of them participate and the resulting young will be a phoenix, like mommy.

With us… I guess it will be a surprise.

Not that it's time to think about that. Things aren't on the right track yet. Not all the way, anyway.

Deciding to take a step toward rectifying that, I grab a couple of the candles out of the living room and take them into the bedroom. The nightstands on either side of the bed seem like the logical place to set the mood.

Not that we need ambiance…

But Keyla deserves a bit of romance. A lot happened and she didn't get a choice in much of it. I think she deserves to be courted and swept off her feet a little, even if it's after the fact.

After lighting the candles, I turn down the sheets and pull some supplies out of my duffle. I managed a side trip to the pharmacy when we were at the Travon med clinic and picked up some condoms, lube, almond oil for massage, and some sweet treats.

What can I say? I'm a bit of a teddy bear.

My bear's heightened hearing pricks as I capture the soft sound of footsteps approaching from behind. The quickening of blood pumping in my veins is silly. I'm not a horny teenager trying to get lucky.

Why do I feel like one?

"Got something in mind for the evening, Bear?"

My eyes roll closed as Creed presses up behind me. Strong arms wrapped around my ribs as the male nips my neck. "Keyla's not back from across the hall yet, but Kotah and Calli just left, so I'm sure she won't be long."

"Good. I'm looking forward to unwinding. We've been on the move for days. I think we need to relax and get back to the three of us bonding."

Creed's hand drops down my front and he unbuttons the front of my jeans. "Three? Rhylan isn't included in this plan of yours?"

"I paid him a visit and invited him, but he's twisted up about his brother and the decisions he's made. He needs a night on his own to decompress."

"I respect that. Thank you for including him."

As a reward, he slides his hand into my pants and palms the length of my quickly stiffening cock. I flex my spine, pressing tight against Creed's groin.

The deep-throated groan he lets off makes me smile. "I made it clear what I had planned and told him to join us if he changes his mind."

"I appreciate you looking forward to getting us alone together. Up for more torture, are you?"

"If the torture you're offering is more of the delicious penetration and rough riding of our last session the answer is a definite yes."

I turn, caged between Creed's embrace and the footboard of his massive paneled bed. The male is tall and broad, and I relish how our physical connection affects him: the scent of his arousal, the anticipation dancing in his dark eyes, the unmistakable bulge filling out the front of his pants...

It's all so fucking hot.

Creed has an alpha dominant streak and when he grips my clothes and starts to strip me down, that's fine by me. Jeans and boxers get shoved down the muscled trunks of my thighs and pool at my ankles. My shirt is next. He yanks it up my ribs and over my head, discarding it onto the floor.

"Keyla didn't mind catching up the last time she caught us together, so I say we get things started."

I step out of my clothes and grunt as I'm shoved back and my ass bumps against the footboard. "No, she didn't mind. By her scent that night, she loved it. Our girl is more than a little sexually curious."

"I love that she's adventurous." Creed unbuttons his shirt and lets it hang open, putting those rows of muscled abs on display. He unbuckles his belt, and his slacks drop to the floor next to mine.

As usual, he's free balling it under his fancy pants.

So, hot.

Before he starts getting hot and heavy, I ease my fingers under the fabric of his shirt and stroke the scarred flesh on his back. "You don't need to hide a part of yourself from us. We've got you. Whatever the pain is, you're safe with us."

He swallows and dips his chin. "I know... and I appreciate that. May I leave bearing my soul to another night? As you said, it's been a busy few days and we need to reconnect."

I lean forward and brush his lips. "That's what being safe is all about. There's no wrong answer. You decide what to share and when. Just know that it won't change anything. We're building something great here."

Creed's smile softens and he kisses me back. The guy is usually wild and a little aggressive, but there are these moments, few and far between, where I see the softer, more vulnerable side in him.

I understand why he doesn't show that side much. Growing up a prince and now the king of a war-torn world, I'm sure vulnerable wasn't an option.

His mouth seals over mine as his hands cup my jaw. The kiss is tender, and I get the feeling he's sharing a part of himself he doesn't expose often. I'm honored.

Easing back, he offers me a genuine smile. "Thank you for being you, Bear. I understand why Keyla refused to give you up. You are an incredible man."

When he drops to one knee and looks up at me, my cock twitches forward in anticipation of what I think is coming next. "I took over last time. Are you good if I take charge again?"

"With me, yeah. I'd like to shift to sensual and sexy with Keyla though. I'm hoping to romance her tonight. You know... slow things down and dig deeper."

"All right. You and I can take the edge off then and slow things down after."

"Sounds perfect. Thanks."

Gripping my cock at the base, he parts his lips over my crown and sucks me into the hot depths of his mouth. My breath hisses from my lungs.

I grab the wooden frame of the bed behind me and brace myself. The suction is amazing and when he scores his teeth along the soft flesh sheathing the solid shaft, I'm pretty much seeing stars.

Creed is an aggressive lover.

I've seen him gentle with Keyla once but other than that, he's pretty hard core. "Tell me if I'm too rough."

"Don't worry about me. I'm a big boy."

He pops off the swollen head of my cock and grins up at me and winks. "Yes, you are."

I curse as he resumes. "Life with you won't be boring, I am certain of that."

In answer, Creed's body releases a wave of dark promise. The scent of his arousal has changed since the mating. It is as glorious and spicy as ever, but now it also carries the mixed scents of Keyla, Rhylan, and I.

Mmm... and by the time the three of us collapse to the mattress tonight, Keyla and I will be covered in it.

You're mine, Bear, he says directly into my mind. *If you want to dig deeper, know that. Too much was taken from me. Never again. I fight for what's mine and you are mine as much as the others.*

My fingers grip into the silky-soft length of Creed's hair. With my hand on the back of his head, I hold him in place as I rock my hips in lazy pushes of in and out.

Wet suction seals the two of us together and my throat tightens as he moves up and down my shaft.

In and out.

"Fuck that's good. Tell me you love doing that."

He opens up the shared mind-link and I'm hit hard and fast with his sensations. The building of pressure in his balls. The ache of him needing to shove his cock inside me and sate his hunger. The hot rush of blood thundering through his veins.

In and out.

I fight the tingling tide of my release unwilling for this to end. It won't be long though. It's too good to last.

Hot. Slick. Silky.

I'm hungry for your cum, Bear. Feed me.

I don't want it to end, but there's no reason to fight it. This is just the first of many orgasms tonight. Focusing on how good it feels, I let his hunger wash over me.

I let off a throaty grunt as my muscles shudder and the orgasm pushing at the head of my cock breaks free. My hips unhinge, my body jacking forward as I pump hot streams of cum into his mouth.

Fuck me, it's so good.

In the back of my mind somewhere, I worry I'm now creaming straight down the back of his throat but the guy doesn't balk.

Creed devours every ounce I give him, his fingers gripping the flesh of my ass with bruising force. I close my eyes and let the glory of the moment take its course.

So, so, *soooo* good.

As my thundering pulse begins to settle, I fall back against the footboard and lock my knees to keep from assplanting. Creed is a demanding lover but he's also endlessly attentive.

When he straightens to his full height, he offers me that crooked grin of his. Stepping in so we're chest-to-chest, he grips my jaw and pulls me into a soul-searing kiss. I taste the salty aftermath of my cum on his tongue and damn, it triggers another round of hard and horny.

"That was quite a warm-up," I breathe, my voice unsteady. "Thanks for that."

"My pleasure."

I laugh. "No. It was definitely *my* pleasure. Now, how about we go find our girl and get her naked too?"

Keyla

It'll never get old. Walking in and seeing Creed and Dillan lost in a moment of carnal pleasure has become a fantasy fulfilled. Part of me hopes to catch them getting all dark and dirty with one another every time I enter a room. This time, I got lucky.

Unlike last time though, I don't interrupt.

I let them have their moment and watch from the doorway.

They left it open for me to come and join them, and I have every intention of doing that... but not until they have their fun.

I make sure I stay far enough back from the doorway to keep from triggering Dillan's sense of smell. And while I watch, I strip naked and fold my clothes over the back of a blue velvet settee by the door.

After draping a throw blanket over the seat, I take a page out of my mates' book and use the sexual show to fuel my fire. They have each tossed off while watching me have sex. I deserve the same opportunity.

I'm an independent female.

I don't need much prompting to start the keening of sensation from taking hold. Two gentle fingers rubbing circles over my clit brings a rush of ache to my core. It's not enough.

I want to be filled.

I want one or both of them inside me.

Images of how that could work flicker through my mind. Mouth and pussy. Front and back. Both of them in my pussy...

I don't think I can manage that a week after losing my virginity, but it is something I want to try. I bite my bottom lip to keep from making noise and increase the pressure, rubbing harder... faster.

I'm not sure if it's because I'm nineteen or newly sexually active or an effect of the soul-searing or maybe I'm just a horny, kinky chick, but lately, I'm damp and throbbing without any coaxing at all.

Put my mates in front of me, take off their clothes, and have them get busy and I'm wild and randy.

The look on Doc's face as Creed swallows his thrusts is too erotic not to get carried away.

Doc's hand gripping the back of Creed's head isn't forcing his submission, it's ensuring the contact isn't broken. Not when he's so close.

I've shared enough oral orgasms with Doc to know when he's nearing his limit. He's going to release soon.

Sweet powers, it's so sexy.

I swallow as his face distorts and he's coming hard into Creed's mouth. He grunts and stiffens, his abs flexing with every heaving breath.

Closing my eyes, I lock that image in my mind and focus on myself. I'm not as good at this as Doc is. He has such a way with his fingers that I buckle against his touch with ease.

And then there's his mouth... and Creed's mouth...

My nipples ache and I slide one hand up the smooth plane of my stomach to tweak the peaks.

Oh, I need more hands.

"Little Wolf, is there anything we can help you with here?"

I open my eyes and bite my bottom lip. "If it's not too much trouble, yes. I need to be thoroughly devoured and then filled by both of you while I shatter."

Creed grins. "I love a girl that knows what she wants. As it happens, our bear had similar urges and has things set up for a night of fun."

Doc winks, bending down to scoop me up against his broad chest. "True story. The only thing we were missing was the guest of honor—our queen."

Creed

I close the bedroom door all but an inch in case Rhylan does decide to join us. Following Dillan's naked swagger back to the bed is no hardship—our bear has a fine ass—but it hits me that other than the sexual encounter Keyla and I shared on the mental plane, we've relied on a bed.

I make a mental note to expand our experiences now that the castle is ours once again.

Doc sets Keyla at the edge of the mattress, and she scoots back and stretches long, without a hint of modesty. She told me once that wildlings are naked so often due to shifting that nakedness doesn't affect her.

It certainly affects me.

Climbing onto the bed with her, I position myself between Keyla's thighs. "Close your eyes, my queen. I've been looking forward to this for days."

Keyla does exactly as she's told and her trust in me is humbling.

With gentle pressure on the inside of her thighs, I open her up and smile at her glistening folds. "Look at the mess you've made. So wet and slick. You're a hungry little wolf tonight."

"Yes, I am."

"Good. We're hungry too, aren't we, Bear?"

Dillan winks and dips his chin. "Famished."

The feminine whimper she makes, coupled with the arch in her back, does me in. "Do you trust me enough to let me have my way with you without question? I promise everything I have in mind is about your pleasure."

She meets my gaze, her rich, brown eyes wide with excitement. "I trust you."

"Good girl." I lick my lips, my body already thrumming with a need to get at her. "Dillan, would you grab a couple of silk ties from my closet, please?"

"You got it."

Keyla's grin at the mention of the ties is sweet and eager. She truly is agreeable to try anything.

I pause for a beat and take in the sight of her stretched out like a goddess before us. She's gloriously bared to me, and the soft lines of her body steal my soul more every time I'm blessed to see them.

"You're beautiful, Nakeyla Northwood. I am honored to have you as my own."

"As you should be." She grins. "I *am* pretty great."

"Yes you are," Dillan says, returning with the ties. "And we're going to spend the night appreciating you. Tonight, is spoil our queen night."

"Yay! What have I done to deserve such special treatment?"

"You're a special kinda girl," Doc says.

The look on her face is honestly the cutest thing I've ever seen. She's so eager and filled with wonder. Claiming one of the ties, I bind her wrists together and lace the silk tail through the spindles at the top of the headboard to secure her arms over her head. "Tonight, is about you, Keyla—all you."

Doc chuckles. "And a little bit us."

I grin and take another tie. "True. It's no hardship to worship you, but the focus is you."

As I press the silk fabric against her eyes, I meet her gaze. "The mind is a powerful sexual organ. Focus on your senses: the smell of our arousal, the gentle brush of our touch, the sounds of our pleasures, and the taste of our skin. At any point, if you're not enjoying anything we do, I want you to tell us right away."

Her mental energy is so powerfully charged, she's practically bursting with excitement. "Agreed, but I'll love it. I have no doubts about you guys."

"Lift your head so I can tie this." She does, and I secure the tie and blindfold her. Rising to my knees, I assess Doc's needs as well. He's hungry for Keyla too and I don't want him to feel left out. "You're on kisses and nipples for a moment. I need to feed again. Then I'll pass the reins and you can take control. Is that all right?"

"Perfectly. Get your fill."

From beneath lowered lids, I keep my gaze locked on Keyla. I plant my palms on either side of her hips and drop toward her sex.

Fuck she consumes me.

Despite my intention to give her the romance and sensuality I know she deserves, once I get to where I'm headed, I'm overcome with a raw, whipping need.

I grip her hips, pull her against my mouth, and latch onto her core. Lapping her up, I shut out the world and focus on her sensitive flesh.

Initial contact brings a rush of fresh moisture to my tongue, and I swallow it down. The bonded male in me relishes the thought of her cream and Dillan's mingling inside me. It's carnal, slightly primal, and a little crass, but I can't help it.

And as much as it fills me, it's not enough.

By the time this night is through, the silky residue of sex will cover all three of us, inside and out.

I flick my tongue, teasing and penetrating, losing myself in my dedication to coax as much honey from her as possible. The gentle weight of her legs settles over my shoulders and then she's working herself against my chin and mouth. That's my girl. As I said a moment ago...

I love a girl who knows what she wants.

It's still sinking in that she is mine and I get to keep her and claim her forever. And, as good as it is now, it's only going to get better.

When her first orgasm of the night hits hard, her hips buck as her wild side ascends and she calls out my name... twice.

CHAPTER THREE

Rhylan

The morning arrives with a haze of memory and a steady thrum lighting off behind my eyes. *Maybe if I lay here with my eyes closed for another few days I'll feel better.* I breathe deep and my dragon stretches languidly at the feminine scent filling our sinuses.

Keyla.

My sense of surroundings sharpens, and I realize the warm softness cushioning my cheek isn't my pillow… it's fur.

Prying my eyes open a crack, I ready for the assault of daylight and the spearing of daggers into my retina. The pain doesn't come. The drapes are pulled and it's my animal vision that allows me to see.

I'm lying on my side, curled up and spooning Keyla's stunning white wolf. She's sound asleep, her gentle breaths escaping in almost silent whispers. She smells like sex and sated female, and I'm not surprised.

Doc told me exactly what they had planned last night. I'm glad they enjoyed themselves.

I do a gut-check on that thought and yeah... neither man nor dragon wants to kill anyone because they got naked last night with my mate. They had Creed but I'm okay with that. He's mine too. I made that clear. They respect my claim but in turn, I find that I respect theirs.

It does hurt a little that the universe chose Keyla as his perfect other half.

She is Creed's fated mate.

Our mate. My dragon pushes the thought at me with force. *Our beautiful queen.*

I'll never argue about Keyla's beauty—no one with eyes could —but she's young and idealistic and doesn't understand the kind of baggage being claimed by a male like me means.

Afraid to wake her, I remain perfectly still. I'm not ready to confront the mixed feelings I have for her. Part of me wants to grasp hold of everything she offers—acceptance, understanding, and a safe place where people of worth honor and love me.

Another part of me doubts she knows what she's talking about.

Another part of me resents her place at Creed's side.

Another part of me is thankful she came along and set Creed's world right.

I could think myself into circles all day long.

She wakes. My dragon pushes to the surface, eager to interact. I don't share that enthusiasm.

But he's right. Keyla is waking, her muscled shoulders twitching, her fur pulling under my fingers. When her eyes open, I expect her to shift to her human form.

Then what will I do?

She doesn't. She glances over her shoulder, catches me watching her, and lays her head back down. When she closes her eyes again, I smile. All right then.

The boys must've worn her out because she's certainly not ready to get up.

Honestly, now that I think about it, I'm not either. Closing my eyes again, I allow myself one caressing stroke over her shoulder and down the thick pelt of velvety white to her back legs.

Breathtaking....

I must've fallen back to sleep because the next time I wake, I have Keyla's wolf in my face. I've nuzzled into the fur of her ruff and my twin is backing out of my suite looking murderous.

Easing out of the bed without waking her takes a bit of effort but the moment I'm free, I pull on my boxers and pad up the hall to Vik's suite. He has his bags packed and is pulling on his leather jacket.

"You're leaving?" I step inside his suite and close the door. "I get that things are messed up between us, but don't leave. We'll figure it out."

"When did you start sleeping with the queen?"

"I've never... I'm not. I woke up with her there just now. That's the first time I've gotten anywhere near her and I had nothing to do with it."

"So, Creed's soul-seared mate walked away from the king's bed and let herself into yours? I find that hard to believe. She reeked of sex."

"But not sex with me."

"You expect me to believe you?"

"Believe what you like. You've decided to think the worst of me on all accounts, so even though you can smell that I'm telling you the truth, don't let that sway you from your cutting judgment."

Vik grabs a duffle and slings the strap over his right shoulder and then grabs another and slings it over his left. "You don't get to tell me what to do, Rhy. You're not my brother anymore, remember?"

Those words cut deep, and I let him see the damage it does. "Whether you want to admit it or not, somewhere deep down, you know I did the right thing. We were being blackmailed to destroy our honor. Creed is the rightful ruler. Laryssa was never fit to sit on the Dornte throne."

He grips the handle of his suitcase and shakes his head. "The politics of the quadrant had nothing to do with our duty. Our duty was to our mother and the Silverwing name. You pissed all over it, so I guess it's a good thing you mated him—you can take Thornebane now. Mom and I, however, are fucked."

"Then stay and we'll figure out what to do. We'll get Mom away from Shadowcaster and bring her here. Even pissed at me, you have to see that we're in a stronger position to defend ourselves with my new mates and the Phoenix Quint behind us."

He flips me a middle-fingered salute and walks off.

I follow him out to the hall and curse. He's not listening. He can't see past me mating Creed to anything that might be achieved now that we're free of Laryssa. "Vik. Seriously. You don't have to leave."

He casts a derisive look over his shoulder. "Your mates made it damned clear that anyone opposed to Creed reclaiming the throne needs to vacate the castle."

"But we were never in Laryssa's corner. We were coerced. Creed won't hold you to that."

Vik shakes his head. "Unlike you. I was loyal to Laryssa because I swore an oath. I won't pretend I wasn't just to land on my feet. You consider yourself a man of honor. That's hypocritical. If I were you, I'd take a hard look in the mirror."

Reaching into his pocket, he pulls out something and tosses it to me. "Shadowcaster needed someone to deliver that to you—I volunteered."

I stare at the black and gold disc in my hand and my world comes crashing down around me. "You volunteered to serve me an exile disc? Do you truly hate me enough to relish destroying me and wiping me out of the hierarchy of our people?"

He nods. "I gotta say, it's damned satisfying to see you and your lofty ideals go up in flames. You did this, Rhy, not me. Stop looking like a wounded dog. You're the asshole here, not me."

Creed

I'm finishing in my dressing closet when I hear the door to the corridor open and step out to greet Keyla in the living room. She's not nearly as happy on her return as she was when she left. "Good morning, Little Wolf. How did you and our dragon sleep?"

She sighs. "The sleeping went well... or at least I thought it did. I woke up once and he was watching me. He looked confused but content. When he didn't tell me to get out, I took that as a good sign."

"But?"

"But when I woke up just now, he was gone. No goodbye. No note. Just an empty bed. He couldn't wait to put distance between us, I guess."

I sense her mental anguish and it's not an energy I enjoy. "I doubt that's it. Rhy's a hard guy to get to know but he's also a good guy. I'd be very surprised if he was being overtly rude. There's likely another explanation."

She reaches up on her toes and kisses my cheek. "You're probably right. Let's forget about it."

I hear her words but don't buy into her forced smile.

"There's our beautiful girl." Doc emerges from the bathroom dressed and ready for our day. "How'd it go across the hall? Did Rhy's dragon settle down once you snuggled in?"

"His dragon was happy enough. The man less so." She's losing hold of that weak smile and I feel her emotion pushing to break free. "I don't want to hold us up. Give me ten minutes to shower and get ready for our day."

She doesn't wait for an answer. Ducking her head, she retreats and closes herself into the bathroom.

Doc frowns. "What was that about?"

"I think she's feeling a little snubbed by our dragon. When she woke up, he'd left the suite without a word and she's a little deflated."

Dillan turns toward the exit and strikes off. "I'll show him what a little deflated looks like."

The bear is out the door and across the corridor before I can catch up and grab his shoulder. It takes a great deal of effort to slow down an angry bear, but I manage to get myself between him and Rhylan's door. "How about I talk to Rhy and you check in with Lukas to see if we're still on for today?"

The rumble of his bear's growl tells me what he thinks about that.

"Honestly, Bear, I've got this. Rhylan isn't a mean-spirited person, and we all know he's going through personal stuff with his brood and his brother. Let me check in with him and see what happened."

Doc sighs and takes a step back. "Fine, but if he plans on hurting her on the regular, I will nut-punch him so hard those globes won't ever dare to drop again."

Oh hell. "Understood. I'll express our stance on things and make it clear."

After another moment of hesitation, Doc's muscle-banded shoulders relax, and he stomps down the hall toward the room assigned to Lukas.

I watch him go and chuff. He might be beta in the hierarchy of things but he's alpha possessive of his wolf.

Which is good—great even.

Keyla deserves her men to be committed to raze the world to keep her happy.

I had hoped Rhylan understood that.

A light knock on Rhy's door brings no response, so I use my

powers to probe the mental energy of the room's interior. *Oh, fuck. It's worse than I thought.*

Letting myself in, I close the door behind me and meet the anguished gaze of our dragon mate. He's staring at the black disc in his palm and looks wrecked. "What is that? What happened?"

Rhy launches off the bed and crosses the room looking pissed. He opens the drawer of his cabinet and tucks the disc away. "None of your slecking business. That's what it is."

"Fine. Fuck you. I was just asking."

He pivots and rebounds back at me. "What is it with you three thinking my private space is open for visitors. First the bear last night, then the wolf this morning, and now you. What does a guy have to do to get some slecking alone time?"

I point a finger into his chest and try to reel in my temper. "I just defended you to Doc, saying you're a solid guy that would never hurt Keyla intentionally. If I'm wrong, tell me now and I'll let him come in here to nut-punch you as he planned."

"Why would he want to do that? What did I do?"

"Keyla is hurt that you ghosted her this morning. She did a nice thing and when she woke up you were gone."

"I didn't ghost her. I woke up and Vik was glaring at us from the doorway. I followed him to his room to have it out and when I got back, she was gone."

"That's all it was? You weren't pushing her away? Or snubbing her attentions?"

"No. I don't understand why she was here in the first place but I'm not the kind of asshole that would ghost her to teach her a lesson."

I didn't think so.

"She was here because she sensed your dragon's turmoil from our bed. At four o'clock this morning, she sat up and said your dragon needed comfort. I said I would come to check on you. She insisted it wasn't me he needed. Your dragon craves to be near her."

"I don't know anything about that, but yeah, my dragon was content to have her wolf here when I woke up. Why would she think she needed to get out of bed in the middle of the night and come to me?"

I run my fingers under the blond screen draped in front of his eyes and flip his hair back so he can see me. "I'm not sure. She possesses an amazing level of empathy, like her brother, and she is developing powers we don't yet understand. She said your dragon was restless and needed her. Doc and I didn't argue. Then she came back looking like you kicked her kitten."

Now it's his turn to look confused. "I just went to Vik's room so we could fight in private. It wasn't a commentary on her in any way."

I tilt my head toward my suite. "Maybe take a moment to explain that to her before we begin our day."

His dragon lets off a low growl. "I shouldn't have to apologize. I didn't do anything wrong."

"I'm not asking for you to apologize. I'm saying explain to her what happened. Jaxx told me a human saying the other night, 'A happy wife makes a happy life'. And in this case, it will also keep you from getting nut-punched by an angry bear."

CHAPTER FOUR

Doc

*L*ukas and I find Creed and Rhylan in the hallway outside the dragon's room. I give our fourth a serious once-over laden heavily with stink eye and he meets the hostility. He growls back at me. "I didn't ghost her. I'll go talk to her and explain. Stay away from my nuts."

When he storms off, Lukas casts me a curious glance. "Do I want to know?"

I fight the urge to follow Rhy inside and pound on him. "Likely not. It's mating madness."

The guy winces like I'm talking about a disease that makes your face fall off. Stepping back, he holds up his hands. "That mating madness shit is contagious. Don't give it to me."

I chuckle and gesture to Creed. "It's not all bad. There are perks. Have you met my mate, the King of Dornte? He's pretty fucking great… and pretty great at fucking."

Creed offers me a sexy smirk. "You coming on to me, Bear?"

"Is it working?"

"Maybe. We have a few minutes before we leave."

Lukas rolls his eyes and brushes past us. "No, you don't. Get your mates together and I'll see who's coming from the quint. I think it's only Brant. Kotah and Hawk need to go to Travon to establish the gate coordinates and settle up a few favors Hawk promised last week. Calli and Jaxx said they'd stay with your sister."

When Lukas strides down the hall toward the Auburn Suite to connect with the quint, I follow Creed back inside ours. "What did the dragon say for himself?"

Creed leads the way toward the kitchen while he explains to me how Rhylan woke up with Vik leering at them and then he vacated his bed to go to Vik's room to have it out. Keyla was sleeping, so he didn't disturb her.

"So, it was just bad timing then?"

Creed checks the oven and there is a tray of breakfast quiches the chamber staff brownies left warming for us. "Seems so. We'll let them work it out and see where we end up for the day. Keyla said there were many strained days with the quint while things aligned."

I chuckle. "True story. Brant and Hawk didn't get along at all. Hawk wanted nothing to do with Calli. Jaxx got hissy and pissy with anyone who upset Calli. Everyone loved Kotah, though."

Creed pulls out four glasses and sets them on the island countertop. "It seems impossible not to. Keyla said her brother's omega genes are incredibly rare, but I'd be surprised if she doesn't possess some of the same gifts. Her empathy for others is incredibly strong. I think that's how she knew she needed to go to Rhy this morning."

I see why he'd think that.

Keyla is more than the woman she appears. With each day that passes, there seems to be more greatness budding inside her. I've noticed the omega similarities myself, but there's also been her ability to open mental communication and call the Amberloq power during battle and a bunch of other little things.

Creed pulls the tray of quiche pastry bundles out of the oven when Keyla and Rhylan come in to join us.

"Is everything smoothed out?" I read Keyla's easy smile and am relieved. "You two are sorted, then?"

Keyla comes to me for a hug and then turns to assess the food. "I think all the extra mental energy is making me more sensitive than usual. I'm sorry I caused a scafuffle."

Creed and Rhylan both chuckle.

"What is a scafuffle, Little Wolf?" Creed asks, setting the tray on the counter as he grabs a plate.

"Exactly what it sounds like. An upset. A ripple in the waters."

Creed dishes a couple of breakfast pastries onto plates and slides them toward us.

I find the cutlery drawer and set us up. "Well, I'm glad we're good. We know from experience it makes for a long day of team investigation when people aren't getting along."

Creed chuckles. "That's mine and Rhylan's wheelhouse over the past two years. The two of us mastered hostile tension."

"Past tense," Keyla says. "Now it's sexual tension. That's much better."

He grins. "Much, much better."

Keyla

The four of us finish our breakfast and by the time I'm sliding a few things into a backpack, Lukas arrives and says we're almost ready to roll. I look over the group and think 'ready' might be overstating things.

Rhylan is putting on a good front, but he's hurting and feeling lost and betrayed. He didn't elaborate on what Vikarus said to him this morning, but it cracked the foundation of his world.

Lukas checks his FCO watch and reads an incoming message. "The team leader for the four men watching the witch's building confirms the redhead went into the building last night and has yet to come out. It's safe to assume she either has a lover living there or she lives there herself."

"Has your mating beacon given you any other directions for us to follow?" Rhylan asks.

I focus on the buzz in my blood that has been part of me since the moment I first laid eyes on Creed. In that moment, a lightning bolt of fae energy lit me up from the inside and it is still crackling with power.

It's not nearly as invasive or persistent as it was, but it has never gone away. "It has more to say but not right now. It seems content at the moment."

Creed chuckles. "If you can consider a magical beacon of the universe content."

Doc grins. "It's better than discontent."

"That's very true." I finish with the backpack and Doc slings it over his shoulder. "So, are we ready?"

Lukas leads us back to the main living room and then jogs across the hall to knock on the suite door for the quint. "Roll out, people."

My brother and his mates exit their suite in a rush of joking and chatter. It fills my heart to see them interact as they do. We'll get there. In four months, we'll be as happy as they are.

I believe that with everything in me.

Calli hugs me good morning and Jaxx bends down to kiss my cheek. "Mornin' beautiful. You whippin' these boys into shape?"

I giggle when he winks at me. Jaxx is a flirt and an easy friend to have. I love him to bits. "I'm not sure what kind of shape we're in just yet, but we're getting there... one misunderstanding at a time."

Brant laughs. "Been there, done that."

"And look where you are now."

Calli grins and eyes up my guys. "I have no doubt they're worth the effort."

"Hey, did you cook?" Brant lifts his chin and sniffs the air, his head turning toward the scent. "Whatever you had smells better than what we had."

Creed chuckles and points toward the kitchen. "Help yourself to whatever is left."

"Grab yours to go, Bear," Hawk says. "Kotah and I have a timetable. We're meeting the Prince of Travon in less than an hour."

Creed perks up. "Satune. Good guy. He portrays himself as a bit of a pompous prick, but it's an act. People tend to take advantage of nice guys in this realm, so taking an offensive is often the best way of shutting people with selfish intentions down."

"Good to know," Hawk says. "Then Kotah will do most of the talking. People sometimes take me as a bit of a pompous prick myself, but everyone loves our wolf."

Kotah rolls his eyes and waves away the fawning of the group.

Brant returns with the baking sheet in hand and four quiches left. "Anyone else hungry?"

Calli snags one and holds her hand underneath to catch any crumbs. "Okay, I'm going to check in on my girl. Have a great and successful day. Come home safe and tell us all about it later."

"Will do." Kotah kisses her and then bends to kiss her belly. "Be good for your mama, baby. Your daddies will be back later."

I smile at the sight of my brother gushing over his unborn baby phoenix. I always knew he'd be a great dad but didn't realize it would be so soon.

As long as he does exactly the opposite of everything our parents did with us, he'll win father of the year.

"All right. We're off." Brant kisses Calli next and then Hawk moves in to say goodbye. Once that's taken care of, the eight of us stride through the halls of Thornbane castle and head for the shuttle loop.

"So, we're all going to the portal hub together and then splitting up?"

Hawk nods. "Kotah and I have our meeting with the prince and then a couple of other appointments set up with the gentleman who financed our little raid last week. We're hoping to get everything taken care of today and be back by dinner."

"Do you want me to assign you an escort?" Creed asks. "I realize you're very capable, but you don't know the lay of the quadrants well yet."

"That's true, but I've made arrangements. The liaison for Travon offered himself up as a guide for the day and I accepted. We'll let them lead the way for now and see how that works. We want to get a sense of who we're dealing with."

"Honestly," Creed says, "the leaders of the other quadrants have always been competitive and a little standoffish, but respected and civil neighbors."

"So, where did Laryssa come from?"

"One of the wealthy families living in exile in the fringe. My father had her father removed from the quadrant council for hateful speech against members of our fae races and inciting violence between species."

"And she decided to get even," Rhylan says.

I feel the anguish Creed suffers over that and sense how deeply he mourns his parents—as family, as mentors, and as leaders of the quadrant.

"You'll do them proud," I say, sliding my branded hand into his. Even now with our mating secured, there's still an overwhelming pleasure when our brands connect. "We'll work together every day to live up to their expectations for the quadrant."

Creed winks down at me and squeezes my hand back. *How do you always know exactly the right thing to say to me?*

I pay attention. You're my perfect other half. I know how I would feel at this moment if I were you.

He glances down at me and shrugs his broad shoulders. *You and your brother are in virtually the same situation. When will you tell Kotah about Laryssa and Sebastian poisoning your father to make him king?*

Hawk sent a man back to Pennsylvania last night to instruct his business partner to start gathering proof. Once they finish in Travon, I'll tell him so he can return to our realm and take care of things.

We arrive at the shuttle loop at the back of the castle and two men rush out to wave in a conveyance. The royal shuttle pulls up and we start loading. "Would you like a driver, Majesty?" the concierge asks.

"No, that's fine," Creed says. "We're headed straight to the portal gate. Nothing worth wasting the time for a driver. Thank you, though."

The man dips his chin, and I can tell he's deciding about whether or not to say something more.

"Is something on your mind, Gantley?" I ask, reading his name off his nametag. "You look like you have something to say."

The man blushes and nods. "Only that I'm pleased to have a Thornebane back at the helm of the quadrant. It's been a difficult couple of years. We've missed having your family in power. A great many people were affected by the actions of the usurper queen."

I reach out and squeeze his hand. "There is a saying my father used to tell people in our realm. He'd say, You are not the darkness you suffer. You are the light that endured and survived."

The man smiles up at me. "You are as wise as you are beautiful, my queen."

"Are you flirting with my mate, Gantley?" Creed asks, giving the guy a stern look.

Before the poor man has a heart attack, I chuckle and wave away Creed's words. "He's teasing. You are sweet and we thank you for your thoughts. I look forward to speaking with you again at the staff interviews."

He grins. "As do I. Have a wonderful day."

I wave goodbye as Creed sweeps me up the steps of the shuttle and we take our seats. "Dornte portal hub."

"Dornte Portal hub," the automated voice says. "Estimated arrival time twelve minutes."

And with that, we settle into our seats and begin our first day as rulers of the Dornte quadrant.

∾

Creed

We arrive at the purple building in Clarinta by ten and Lukas directs us into the office tower across the street. Keyla told me Hawk and Lukas would take care of things, but I never expected them to go to these lengths.

Hawk rented a vacant office suite on the tenth floor that overlooks the main entrance of the witch's condominium tower across the street and has a four-man team in place for surveillance on my behalf.

When we arrive, two men leave their equipment at the windows and rise to greet us.

"Is she still in there?" Lukas asks.

The man who comes to shake our hand nods. "Henry is in the parkette at the back of the building reading a book on a bench. Unless she glamored herself to change her appearance, she hasn't exited the front or back of the building."

I stare across the street, my fingers curling into fists. When we were in Clarinta last week, our beacon drew us straight into the witch's path and we followed her to that building. Now, all we have to do is capture her and force her to remove the spells she cast on Honor and me.

"Is everyone clear on the plan?" Lukas asks.

We all nod. We've gone over it a dozen times.

"We've got one shot at this," he says. "My guess is if she gets away, she won't come back for us to take another run at her."

"We'll get her," Keyla says.

"Damn straight." Doc accepts a firearm from Hawk's men and checks the magazine. "Locked and loaded. We'll get her."

"Dead or alive," I say, liking the first option considerably more.

"No. Not dead," Lukas says, his voice tense. "She's a powerful foe. If she won't release the spells voluntarily, which I suspect she won't, I need to study her magical signature to unravel the damage she's done."

All I can picture is her dead.

"Creed? Are you hearing me? If you plan on killing her outright, I'll bench your ass and you can wait here."

I scowl. "You could try. It wouldn't work, but you could try."

Lukas purses his lips and growls. "Why do I always end up helping moody assholes?"

Keyla steps into the standoff and grips my arm. "We understand, don't we? Honor's best chance at recovery is having the Blood Witch captured for Lukas to study. Removing the curses is our priority over revenge, right my love?"

As much as I want to pull away and go murder the bitch across the road, once again, Keyla's soothing touch has tamed the beast in me. "I understand. We need her alive for my sister's sake."

"And yours," Keyla says, reaching to cup my jaw. "You can be free of the beast and restored to the man you were before the raid."

I shake my head. "Even if the curse is removed, I'll never be that man again, Little Wolf."

Her smile is soft and sad. "No. I suppose not. Eyes on the horizon then. Our future is ahead of us."

I nod. "Agreed. We end this and start living our future today."

"Done deal," Lukas says. "Where's the door card?"

His man points to the top of an otherwise empty desk in a vacant cubical. "Henry stole it this morning from a businessman heading off to work. He likely won't realize it's missing and cancel it until tonight."

Lukas collects the purple square and slides it into his pocket. "All right. Rhylan and I will enter the building first, Keyla and Creed are the loving couple coming in next, and Doc and Brant have our six. Got it?"

"Roger that." Doc grabs two empty coffee cups from the floor beside their chairs. "Carry these and you'll blend in. Just two people out to grab some java."

Keyla chuckles. "Creed doesn't really blend. He's six-foot-three guy with ebony eyes and long white hair."

I pull the hood up on the sweater I borrowed from Doc and cover my head. "How about now? Better?"

Keyla laughs. "Now you're six-foot-three with ebony eyes and long white hair under a hood."

Lukas mutters something and passes a hand in front of my face. "It's temporary but will work well enough for what we're doing."

Keyla, Rhy, and Doc are staring.

"What? What did he do?"

"He glamored you to look like an old man," Brant says. "A withered, homely old man."

Keyla rolls her eyes. "Don't believe him. You just don't look like you. You've got black hair and green eyes. It's a fine disguise."

"Pitter-patter," Brant says.

Keyla nods as if she understands what he means. "Let's get atter. Evil witch, here we come."

CHAPTER FIVE

Keyla

*I*t's unnerving to look at Creed and not see the male I know is beneath the illusion of Lukas's glamor. Still, it's safer this way. He is very recognizable as the King of Dornte and if the Blood Witch happened to see him coming our advantage of surprise would be gone.

As planned, Lukas and Rhylan make their way across the street while Creed and I leave the building from another exit so that we come along the sidewalk from another direction.

Lukas thought it would be too noticeable if all six of us came out from the main exit and shot straight across the road. I've learned not to question him.

Lukas is excellent at what he does.

When they head into the glass breezeway of the condominium building, Creed and I pretend to drink our coffees and follow them inside.

I sense Doc's bear close behind us and my wolf ascends, excited for what comes next.

"Thanks so much," I say to Rhylan as he holds the door open

for us. I pretend he's just a helpful stranger and pay it forward, holding the door open for the two handsome bears coming in behind us.

Lukas calls the elevator and while the six of us wait silently for the car to arrive, Creed and I toss our cups in the trash slot provided.

The whine of mechanics signals the arrival of the elevator, and the doors squeak as the pulley system opens them up. Two blue-skinned faeries hurry to catch the elevator, but Brant and Doc turn to face them and fill the entrance.

"Sorry, you'll have to get the next one, ladies," Brant says, his voice deep.

The two seem more mesmerized by Brant than put out at having to wait.

I get that. He's a lot of sexy male to take in.

The moment the doors bump shut, I shift and let my wolf take over. My wildling side is close to the surface, so shifting forms is quick and easy. Sniffing the button panel, I search for the witch's scent.

The silver buttons are so polluted with scents it's impossible to get a solid read on what floor she pushes, but I can discern that she's pushed a button near the middle right.

I only came into contact with her for five minutes on the night we raided the compound in the Travon badlands, but you tend to remember the scent of the women hired to torture and curse your mate.

Skimming my nose over the buttons, I press the three with the strongest trace of her.

"Good girl," Brant says. "Eighteen, twenty-one, twenty-four. We'll narrow it down on foot."

When the elevator opens on eighteen there's a three-foot woman with moss-green skin and tufty brown hair waiting on the other side of the doors. I look at her eye-to-eye and she staggers back.

Doc catches her arm as she stumbles and steadies her. "Are you all right, miss? Don't be frightened. Keyla is a sweet girl. She won't hurt you."

"That's a very big dog. Is that a dog? We're not allowed pets in this building. Who are you? You don't live on this floor." Before she descends into a complete mental spiral, Lukas sets a hand on her shoulder and her expression clears. "It's fine. Have a good day."

"You too," Lukas says, escorting her inside the empty elevator.

When the doors shut, Creed pats Lukas on the shoulder. "Thank you for that. She looked like she might sound the alarms."

Lukas gestures for me to continue. "Princess, the floor is yours."

I pad along on all fours and sniff my way up the hall to the left and back and then to the right. With my nose against the tile floor, I'm smelling an overwhelming roar of citrus disinfectant… which is great for the tenants but not great for tracking down an evil witch.

At each doorway, I smell the threshold and the doorknob before moving to the next.

When I'm done, I am satisfied there's nothing here that will lead us to the witch. I sit on my haunches and shake my head. *Not on eighteen.*

"Twenty-one then," Brant says, thumbing the call button. We stand there waiting for a moment and then Doc tilts his head toward the stairs. "Quicker and easier."

Everyone seems to agree. After climbing the three flights of stairs, I repeat my search.

Nope. *Not twenty-one either.*

The moment we exit the stairwell onto the twenty-fourth floor, I let off a little yip. Her scent is present and strong. I don't bother with the tile floor and focus on the threshold and the doorknobs. I find the one I'm sure she's in, but continue until I eliminate the others.

When I return to the entrance to 2408, I shift back and straighten next to my mates. With a nod, I point to the door and step back as Brant and Lukas assume first position.

"Drop the glamor," Creed whispers to Lukas. "When that bitch sees us rushing in, I want her to know it's me coming for her."

Lukas moves his hands in front of Creed's face and then my mate is himself again.

"I missed your face," I whisper.

Creed winks. "That's nice to know."

Lukas turns his attention back to the doorway and I sense when the air crackles to life with the power of his magical abilities. He's working on something and then it becomes clear. As he continues with his magic, the door starts to glow with magical beams that look much like laser beams in a museum.

The warding is extensive and takes almost ten minutes of Lukas's full focus before the beams dim and disappear.

Brant holds out his knuckles for a bump and Doc and I do the same.

Creed and Rhylan seem unaccustomed to the practice but now that the quint is part of their lives, they'll get used to it.

Lukas nods to Brant, and then my brother-in-law pulls out a hand-held thermal gauge to scan the rooms inside. We all lean over his shoulder to look. There are two heat signatures inside and to the left.

One sitting. One lying flat at waist height.

Lukas stands back, draws his weapon, and shows Brant three fingers.

Three, two, one...

∼

Creed

Brant kicks the door with a solid strike of his boot and the slab flies inside unable to withstand the force. Rhylan and Lukas take point. Brant and I are inside next, and Doc and Keyla take position guarding the door to prevent escape.

The Blood Witch looks up from where she's torturing her next poor victim. The woman is stretched out stiff and hovering in the air over the dining room table. The strangled noises she makes are pitiful. They cross between a weak gasp and a sob.

Emaciated as she is, it looks like her life is all but drained from her.

Lukas squeezes off a couple of quick shots before the witch can get her hands up to defend. The force of human bullets is nothing she's prepared for.

Her body twists as first her shoulder is impacted and then her leg. She lets off a demented scream and the woman levitating crashes to the table below.

Rhylan and Brant rush forward but a pulse of magical energy detonates, and we're all thrown back by an invisible wave.

My ears ring as I scramble onto my knees and look back to make sure Keyla isn't hurt.

She and Doc seem dazed but unharmed.

Something wild and primal ignites in me and it gives me the strength to get to my feet and tackle the bitch before the others. I've never struck a woman but for her, I make an exception.

With a hard right cross, I connect and send her head pivoting to the side. Two years of fury and anguish emerge and there's no way I can stop the outpouring of violence. And I don't want to.

"Kill me and your sister never wakes," she grunts.

I barely hear the words when I'm caught up from behind and Brant and Doc pull me off her.

"Creed," Doc grunts as I turn my fury on them. "Let Lukas

take her into custody. Alive is better, remember? We can't condemn your sister."

Lukas moves in, taking advantage of my immobilization. "I'll bind her. You can kill her after I free Honor."

"She needs to die," I seethe.

Keyla blocks my vision and cups my jaw in her hands. A calming rush washes through me, taking the violence out of my fury, much like when her brother touches me. "First we break the spells cursing you and Honor. Then you get your revenge."

I'm practically vibrating with the need to strangle that bitch, but I hear the wisdom in Keyla's words. Reining in my homicidal impulses, I stop fighting the hold of the bears. "All right. I understand. I'm okay."

Keyla's smile is the balm to the fire raging in my soul. She steps forward and meets me chest-to-chest. Her embrace is strength and love and everything I need at this moment.

Over her shoulder, I watch as Rhylan and Lukas struggle to secure the witch. Even bleeding and after a few pounding punches, she's still fighting. The two of them modified a magic inhibitor collar to latch around her neck but she seems to be repelling it somehow.

Lukas is speaking in tongues and the witch is writhing, bleeding heavily out of the wounds in her shoulder and thigh.

"Give it up," I snap. "You're done. Face it and accept your fate."

"Release the dark power you're holding onto," Lukas says. "It's killing you. Surely you feel your body eating itself alive from within."

The scarlet-haired witch smiles at him. "The only way to truly rise to the top is to risk more than others believe is safe."

"You're not on top," I shout. "You might have fooled yourself into thinking so for the past couple of years, but that's over. Accept that you're beaten."

She lets off a maniacal laugh and I'm back to wanting to rip her head off.

Keyla grips my arms hard and gets between me and the woman who leveled my life. "Ignore her. Once that collar is activated, she'll be helpless to fight. Let's see if there's anything we can do for the female."

Shit. I completely forgot about the woman.

Doc hasn't. The healer in him is already hard at work assessing her injuries. When we move closer, he meets our gaze and shakes his head.

I understand. There's nothing any of us can do for the female.

Doc steps back looking distraught. "I can't even... I don't even know what was done to her to bring her to this state."

Lukas glances our way and frowns. "It's a desiccation spell. The witch has physically sucked the life force and power out of her to consume and increase her own strength."

"Can it be reversed?" Keyla asks. "Is there a spigot or something to tap the bitch and put it back?"

Lukas shakes his head. "Unfortunately, no. For the female to be that withered and gaunt, the witch has probably been feeding off her for years. The kindest thing we can do is end her suffering."

Fucking hell.

Another casualty of misplaced power.

"What kind of fae is she?" Keyla asks.

I take a good look at her and can't tell. The damage is unbelievable. As horrible as it's been to be cursed and suffer the siphoning of my soul each time I become the beast she cast over me, this is worse—so much worse.

The drained husk of the female tells me nothing of her species, so I scan her with my mind guardian energy. Her comprehension is foggy, her brain activity weak.

Still... I recognize the signature.

My knees buckle. *No. It's impossible.*

But I'm not wrong—it's her.

Rising up, my vision goes red as the world narrows to a pin-dot. "You vile, horrific, bitch." The control I'd barely tethered myself with dissolves in an instant. The scream that roars from my throat is filled with betrayal and fury.

Somehow, the next events seem to happen both in slow-motion and all at once.

I launch to attack and Lukas and Rhylan lose focus. The Blood Witch pushes back in an explosion of power and blasts through the glass of the window behind her.

She can't escape... and yet that's what's happening.

I reach the ledge, diving out to grip her foot or wrist or something to keep her from getting away but it's too late. With a soulless grin, she plummets backward toward the street twenty-four floors below.

Fine. Let her die that way.

But she doesn't.

The air below her glows iridescent, snaps with energy, and then swallows her into nothingness. One moment she's there, dropping toward the street, and the next there's a snap of magic and she's gone.

"Noooo!" I scream.

The beast inside me pulls at my control and I fight not to lose myself to its evil possession. How did this happen? We had her. *I* had her.

"You should've let me kill her!" I have my hands around Lukas's throat. "You let her get away!"

Voices bombard me from all sides, but I don't hear the words. I've got nothing but the darkness of the beast inside me and the rage of knowing the woman who took everything from me is laughing and free.

A bolt of energy hits me and I'm flying through the air. I hit the sofa and flip backward ending up face-first on a carpet.

Before I can get up, crushing weight lands on my back and I'm pinned to the floor.

"We didn't *let* her do anything," Rhylan says, leaning close to my face. "Even with two bullets in her, me holding her, and Lukas trying to undo her magical safeguards, she had enough strength to fight us off. She's a slecking force, Creed."

Keyla lays beside me and brushes my hand. "It's going to be all ri—"

"Don't." I pull my hand away from the comfort of her touch and glare over my shoulder. "Get the fuck off me."

Dillan and Brant exchange a look and then get up.

I push off the floor and focus on the woman dying on the table. My adrenaline flags and my legs threaten to give out. I lean against the wood surface and brush back her hair. It's so much longer than the last time I saw her.

"For two years I have mourned your death and now I wish that had been your end instead of this."

Bloom. My beautiful, spirited lover. I am so sorry.

Her eyes are fogged over with confusion, death closing in, but when she sees me, her gaze brightens a little. *My prince. I knew you'd come.*

I'm sorry. I was held captive and...

Don't... You came... That is everything. Return me home to my family so I may join them in the grove.

I will. I swear.

Then I am at peace for the after.

Knowing what she's saying, I blink back tears. *Blessed be, my beautiful, Bloom.*

Blessed be, my prince.

I swipe at the moisture blurring my vision and meet Lukas's gaze. He's furious with me and has ugly bruising on his throat where I attacked him only moments ago. "I apologize for losing my mind. Please don't take that out on her. She's ready. Please make it quick."

Lukas touches her forehead, whispers a few words in tongues, and then Bloom is gone.

I meet the compassionate gazes of the people I consider my family now and I don't know how to explain. The guilt. The regret. The horror of knowing I've been happy the past week and in love while Bloom lay here bound and dying.

Removing the restraints from her stick-thin wrists and ankles, I scoop her against my chest and head for the door. "It should never have ended like this."

❧

Rhylan

Slecking hell. Vikarus and I fought in the siege of the castle during Laryssa's coup and weren't part of the queen's guard until the castle was secure. I never met Bloom. Creed spoke of her often, but he believed she was dead, and I assumed he was right.

The reality is barbaric.

Creed heads toward the exit with the shell of his ex-lover in his arms and Keyla and Doc fall in behind him.

I'm about to join them when Lukas raises his chin and catches my attention. "Go with them. Brant and I will call our team in and see if there's anything here we can salvage. We'll be back tonight to fill you all in on what we find."

"Good luck.

It's a somber group waiting by the elevators when I catch up. Creed is staring straight at the polished, metal doors and when Keyla sets her hand on his shoulder, he shrinks away from it. "Please don't."

The acrid burn of that rejection singes my nostrils and offends my dragon. Creed's withdrawal cuts her deeply. Dillan reaches to hold her hand, his expression murderous.

Creed's hurting. They understand that, right?

How do they expect him to deal with his feelings for one love by accepting comfort from another? It's messed up. Even from beyond the grave, Laryssa destroys lives.

This isn't Creed's fault. Nor is it Keyla's.

I smell the anguish behind her tears and her silent sorrow affects not only my dragon. I reach forward and brush her tears with my thumb. "We'll make this right. We can't allow that bitch to win."

Keyla lifts her chin and forces a smile. "I'm fine. We were expecting fallout. We just—"

Creed rounds on us, his expression wild. "Bloom *isn't* fallout."

Keyla's wolf lets off a pitiful whine and before I realize what I'm doing, I pull her against my chest. Meeting his gaze, I straighten to my full height. "We all get that your world just exploded. Don't shit on us for caring. Lock it down and back the hell off."

The elevator car arrives, and the doors whisper open. Creed steps into the back of the space. We follow him inside. Doc punches a thumb against the button for ground and the doors shut us in.

Slecking hell.

CHAPTER SIX

Keyla

*R*hylan hails a car for us and it's a bit awkward figuring out who will sit where. Creed slides into the back seat and rests Bloom's body on the seat next to him. Since he's having a hard time looking at me, I take the front seat with Rhy and let Doc take the back.

When we arrive back at the Clarinta Portal hub, we exit the gate for Dornte as a group, and then Creed stops outside one of the doors leading to a local portal. "Rhylan, take Keyla and Dillan back to the castle. I need to handle this alone."

"No," I say, emotions thick in my throat. "The entire point of being mated is you *don't* have to handle things alone. We are here for you. Let us share your burden."

Creed doesn't look at me. He keeps his gaze locked on Rhy. "Please. Get them home safely."

My heartache burns hot but not as hot as my rising temper. Lifting my chin, I push back my shoulders. "You don't get to ignore me while at the same time tell me what to do. We're supposed to be equal partners. That's not what you want right now so fine, consider me stepping back. Rhylan, I would feel better if you escort Creed and ensure his safety. Doc and I are capable of making it back to the castle on our own."

Rhylan looks from me to Doc and back again. "If you're sure."

"I don't need a babysitter," Creed snaps. His voice carries and a couple of people walking by turn to see what's got the king worked up.

I open up a mental channel and meet his gaze. *You're the fucking King of Dornte. Only days ago, you remained a captive of Laryssa. I don't give a flying fuck how badly you want to get away from me. You're indispensable. Take Bloom to her people. Work through whatever you need to work through, and when you're done, we'll be here for you.*

I turn on my heel and strike off toward the exit. Before I get twenty feet, I feel Creed's mental energy brushing my mind. He's angry and twisted up and hurting. *I'm sorry, Little Wolf.*

Yeah. So am I.

I don't stop. I don't turn around. I don't look back.

I can't.

My heart is cleaved in two and the regret in Creed's gaze is enough to do me in.

Queens don't cry in public.

Creed

As Keyla's anguish grows more distant, everything in me wants to call her back to apologize. She's been so good to me. I told her about Bloom, and she was wonderful. I showed her my memories drawer and she supported me. But having her support me through Bloom's death and delivering her to her family...it's too much.

"You hurt her." Rhylan is staring at me, his disapproval plain. "You could've asked her to step back or explained what you needed but you chose to hurt her."

I start walking for the portal that leads to Llewayin. "I didn't *choose* to hurt her. I didn't choose any of this."

Rhy says nothing more on the matter until we leave the Dornte hub and are standing in the lush tropics of the earth guardian's domain. "I didn't know. You might not believe me after what happened with your mother, but I honestly didn't know about Bloom."

The truth of his words is obvious even without using my abilities. Since he drank from me and claimed me as his mate, his mental energy has been wide open to me. I didn't think he'd be involved in something so vile, but it's good to hear.

"I believe you. Please wait for me out here."

Leaving Rhylan at the gate of the earth fae nature preserve, I drop my chin as I approach the sentry. The guard looks at me and then Bloom in my arms and seems to be at a loss. "Majesty?"

"Please lead the way to Lily and Terran of the Great Oak. I return to them their beloved daughter, Bloom."

The sentry looks at Bloom's frail body in my arms and frowns. "Of course. Please, follow me."

When Bloom and I were dating, we were forced to keep our relationship a secret. The crowned prince and a member of the castle staff, even if she was a member of the upper court, was nothing that held any future.

Still, she brought me here once to share her world and her parents with me. Being back here, under these circumstances, is devastating.

"King Creed?" Terran of the Great Oak is a tall, willowy man who wears a laurel of branches, as is the custom for an elder of the Sacred Grove. "What is this?"

I swallow past the obstruction in my throat and force myself to be the man Bloom needs me to be. "Terran, my friend. Today, when I sought out the Blood Witch who aided Laryssa these past years, I found that she had been keeping Bloom prisoner to steal her vitality."

"Bloom?" The man looks at the woman in my arms and is wholly confused. "You believe this waif is my daughter?"

"I am bereft to tell you she is. Before she passed, we shared a few words. Her parting wish was for me to bring her home to her grove."

Running footsteps approach from deeper in the forest and Lily, Bloom's mother, joins us. The woman's beauty, so similar to her daughter's, shatters my already broken heart. "Lily. It is my pleasure to see you again, as well as my deepest regret."

Before I say anything more, Terran steps forward and takes Bloom's body from my arms. "If you don't mind, Majesty. I'd like to be alone with my wife."

I lower my gaze and step back. "Of course. If you ever need anything of me, please do not hesitate to seek me out."

I turn to leave when I remember the pendant around my neck. Stopping, I reach under my shirt and pull it out. It takes me a moment to get the clasp undone and the pendant off, but then I offer it to Lily. "In my years of capture, my memories of your daughter kept me sane. Bloom will always hold a significant place in my heart."

Before I say too much or upset them more, I set the pendant in Lily's hand and take my leave. "Blessed be."

Rhylan is standing, as stoic as ever on the other side of the gate. When I exit, he falls into step with me and frowns. "I truly am sorry for your loss."

I nod, not wanting to think about that right now. "Me too."

"Are we headed back to the castle?"

I consider that for a moment. I need to face Keyla and apologize. I need to start taking control of my castle and my quadrant. I'm in no frame of mind to do either.

"No. I need a drink."

Doc

Keyla and I soon realize we don't have the access credentials to call a private car, so we hop on a public shuttle bus. "Does this bus go to Thornebane Castle?" I ask the navigation screen.

"Thornebane Castle is stop twelve on the current route," the automated voice replies.

"Good enough. Thanks." I scan the rows of seats and head toward two open spots near the back. They aren't together, but they're one in front of the other, so that's okay.

When I get closer, I assess the passengers already seated. I'm about to slide in beside the hairy dude with fifty little spikes sticking out of his cheeks when the woman next to the other vacant seat behind him gasps. "Queen Thornebane. Prince Baskins. Please, allow me to move so the two of you may sit together."

She jumps out of her seat like her ass is on fire and backs up in the aisle to give us space to slide in.

"Thank you," Keyla says. "That's very kind of you."

"Of course, Milady." She drops her gaze, a peach blush warming her pale-yellow skin.

There's a general buzz on the bus now and people are turning and starting to gawk. "Sorry to disturb you, folks," I say, raising a hand. "Don't mind us. We're just heading back to the castle and realized we don't have one of those ID chips you use for transit."

Someone at the front taps the nav screen and frowns. "Shall I reprogram the route to make the castle a priority stop?"

"Oh, no." Keyla lifts her hand to pause the rerouting. "All of you have your schedules to keep. We're in no rush. We're happy to take in the sights until we arrive back home. Thank you, though. We appreciate your thoughtfulness."

I wait until she slides into the window seat and then assess the passengers behind us before sitting down. Funny. I've always been protective of Keyla, knowing she's the princess of our realm, but Queen of Dornte Quadrant puts an even bigger target on her head. It has my bear pacing and a bit growly.

Not that it takes much to make my bear growly.

After a moment though, everyone's curiosity seems to fade enough that we're simply two people on the bus. That helps calm my protective instincts. I want to talk to her, but not with people listening to our mate business. "Will you open a channel for me? I'd like to speak privately with you."

Keyla smiles and takes my hand.

I feel the mental connection open up between us and smile. *You're an absolute marvel. Do you know that?*

And you're a hopeless flirt and much too deeply in love to be objective.

I chuckle. *You can't fault a guy for loving his mate too much.*

Keyla's gaze clouds over with a sad shadow. *No, you can't.*

Her rich, chocolate brown eyes have always been expressive. They project her mood without error: her joy, her confusion, or like now... her heartache. *What was that about with Creed? I feel like a jackass asking but I'm also the only one who doesn't seem to know what's going on. Who was that woman?*

That was Bloom, the earth fae he was in love with when Laryssa seized the castle. He saw her struck down in the battle before he was dragged off by Laryssa's men. He thought her to be dead and mourned her murder for the past two years.

Shit. And he had no idea she'd been captured and tortured for all this time?

Not until he recognized her in the witch's condo.

My bear reels at the thought. If that were me and Keyla was lying a hair's breadth away from death when I found her, I'd lose my mind too. The guilt of not protecting her... of moving on while she suffered... of her being targeted because of me in the first place...

Well, that explains a lot. His guilt and fury are understandable. He must be tangled up in his head and heart so badly he can't even think.

I know, but what hurts is that he wouldn't even look at me. What does that mean?

I lace my fingers with hers and squeeze. *It means he's wrecked that he failed her and moved on to fall in love with you. It'll take him time to process that. He's a proud male and an alpha. The situation is messed up enough that it's shaking his foundation.*

She nods and leans against my chest. *I know. I just wish he could've let me help him through it.*

I shake my head. *Not this time, beautiful. To turn to you would only compound his guilt. Give him time.*

She blinks her tears away, refusing to let them fall. *Luckily, mated for life means we have lots of time.*

True enough.

Keyla

My heart is breaking for Creed and Bloom. To have their lives invaded so brutally. To be tortured and lied to for nothing but power—political and physical. The damage Laryssa and the Blood Witch have inflicted on the realm is terrible.

I make a mental note to speak with Shadow when we return to the palace to face Raven. The realm empathic counselor offered me, and countless others, comfort and sage advice when my father was declining.

Maybe he could help Creed.

He is a talent for not only leading individuals toward finding peace but communities as well.

Dornte could use a man like him to begin the healing process.

I'm still thinking about that when the bus slows for its next stop. We're in a downtown area similar to where Creed and I slept our first night in the realm. The ache in my chest eases a little as I remember the warmth and kindness shown to us by Coal and the underground clan of faery outcasts and unwanteds.

They had so little yet never hesitated to share their food and hospitality with us. I must reach out and ensure they have what they need to thrive now that the quadrant is once again under Thornebane rule.

The bus hasn't start off again and I straighten in my seat to see what's holding things up.

"Street bandits," a woman at the front shouts.

Dillan grabs the seat ahead of us and stands at the same moment four men enter the bus. Two come in from the front door and two from the back door on our right.

They look like homeless hoodlums wearing worn, grungy rags. I recognize the colorful smears marking their cheekbones, brows, and bald heads almost immediately. Creed and I ran into a group like this on the train when we first arrived.

They eyed us up to cause trouble, but Creed forced them back with the threat of his blaster.

Only we don't have a blaster now.

Do you still have the gun Lukas gave you?

Doc frowns. *I do, but with this many people in an enclosed space, it's too dangerous. Innocent civilians are liable to get hurt.*

Good point. *Okay, what do we do?*

He seems to consider that for a moment and then inhales. *Coordinated attack. Do you see that burly guy on the aisle in the fourth row and the tall elf on the opposite side a few rows back?*

I scan the people quickly and find the two he mentioned. *I see them.*

You can tell by the way they're readying to launch that they've got fight in them. Open a connection and tell them to take the man closest to them on my mark.

I'm not sure I have that much control. I don't even know them.

You're stronger than you think and knowing them doesn't matter. You can do this. I have no doubt.

Well, that makes one of us.

Focusing forward, I sift through the mental energies of the people on the bus and try to hone in on the two men Doc pointed out. Then, I open a pathway between us, bringing in Dillan.

To the burly man in the fourth row and the elf in the sixth, this is Queen Keyla in the back. Please nod once to confirm you're hearing this.

My heart skips a beat for the moment it takes before each of them drops their chin to their chest.

I'm hearing you, the big man says.

Me too, says the elf.

You're amazing. Doc says, winking at me. *Okay, boys, are you game to fight back?*

Can't wait.

Yes. Definitely.

Excellent. Is there anything about these fae and their powers we need to worry about?

No. They're hoodlums. Street bandits are fae who don't have enough magic or skills to make a life here without breaking the laws and using force.

Okay, on my mark, Keyla and I will take the back two and you will each take the man closest to you. The two of us have the advantage of seeing all four at once, so we'll call the start, understood?

When they agree, I focus on the two at the back of the bus. They have almost finished looting the people behind us and are moving up the aisle to rob us next. The ones at the front are making their way back, as well.

Almost there, Dillan says. *Hold. Hold. Go!*

Dillan launches out of his seat and tackles his guy down the steps and out the back door. I use the moment of surprise to shift to wolf and lunge at the second man. Biting and clawing, I disarm him and topple him to the aisle. Once he's on the ground, I grab a mouthful of clothing and drag him off the bus as well.

The moment we hit the asphalt, I shift back to fight. My strongest offense is my ability to kick effectively. I wasn't able to do that on the bus, but out here on the concrete pad of the bus stop, it takes me no time before I've delivered a devastating roundhouse to my opponent's head and knocked him out cold.

Dillan has his guy finished too and jumps back on the bus.

A moment later, he steps off with the burly guy and the elf, dragging the last two street bandits with them.

"Taking out the trash," I say, jazzed after the fight. Raising my palm to the air, I knuckle-bump Doc and then move toward the other two. They don't seem to understand at first, so I lift their hands and show them. "That's how it's done, boys. Thanks for your help."

Bending down, I scoop the cloth sack full of cardholders, tablets, and other personal effects and hold it out to the elf. "Would you mind taking that back onto the bus and helping everyone recover their belongings?"

"Of course, Majesty."

Watching him climb back up the steps into the bus, I realize there are dozens of people with their datapads raised, recording us. I wink to the cameras and smile. "Nothing a little Dornte teamwork can't handle. To all the rebels, thieves, and corrupt citizens who thrived during Laryssa's brief stay, your days are over. Pack your bags or change your ways because Dornte isn't your playground any longer."

When I turn back to our captives, I'm pleased to see two duty officers in uniforms securing the hands of the men and shoving them into the back of a police van.

"It seems our job here is done," I say to Doc and the burly

guy. "I guess we should get back on the bus. We're delaying everyone's day."

The burly man chuckles. "I think it's safe to say you two have *made* everyone's day, Majesty."

I grin. "That's sweet. The truth of the matter is that everyone should feel safe in their home. We won't stop fighting until that's Dornte's reality once again."

CHAPTER SEVEN

Rhylan

I've seen Creed angry before. I've seen him wrecked and self-destructive. I've never seen him like this. As we sit in the shadows of the back of this bar, he's crashing into an abyss of anger and self-loathing. I understand completely but how do I help him when I'm not sure how to navigate it myself?

"We're quite a pair," I say, raising my glass to toast us. "The mulch and mash of men left in the wake of Laryssa's treachery."

Creed tips his drink back and I watch his throat flex as he guzzles the burgundy haze down like it's water. When the glass is empty, he slams it down on the pitted wood table and pushes off the bench seat. "Another. I've gotta piss."

I roll my eyes thankful there's nobody within earshot to notice our king's behavior. As hard as I tried to wrangle him back to the castle to wallow in private, he insisted on hitting the first bar we came to.

Thankfully, it's not the kind of place to gather a large crowd in the middle of the afternoon... which I suppose is closing in on evening now.

Damn. How long have we been here?

The crowd of empty glasses littering our tabletop doesn't bode well for making it home unscathed. He's been pounding them down for too long and with much too much enthusiasm. Now we are solidly in public intoxication territory.

Our server is a rough-around-the-edges half-drow with an ink fetish. When she returns with two more glasses of haze, I curse under my breath. "You can stop bringing drinks now. He's had enough."

She lifts a shoulder and rolls her eyes. "Maybe if you were the king I'd stop, but you're not. When my king says to keep them coming, you better believe that's what I'm going to do."

Perfect. Thanks for nothing.

I glance down the back hall toward the bathrooms and wonder what's taking so long. Hopefully, he hasn't clocked out with his cock out. That would be an amazing news story for his first week on the throne.

I pull out my credits card and point to her scanner. "Call up our bill. I'm paying out. If you bring anything beyond those two last drinks you don't get paid for them. Are we clear?"

Her lip curls as she rolls her eyes. After scrolling through her data scanner, she holds it out for me to read. *Ouch. Slecking hell, Creed's paying me back for this.*

I tap my card and the credits are exchanged. When that's taken care of, I slide my card back into its holder and then into the inside pocket of my leather jacket.

There's still no sign of Creed's return, so I head back. Thankfully, instead of open, public washrooms, this bar has six private rooms.

Drawing a deep breath, I sort through the aromas of greasy pub fare and booze and search for the rich, dark scent that is Creed. After assessing the six doors, I knock on the last one on the right. "You fall in?"

"Fuck off. I'm not in the mood for your mouth."

I try the handle and sigh. "Well, I'm not in the mood to shout through a door. If you're done pissing, come back and sit down."

The door to the washroom opens and Creed grabs the front of my shirt. Pulling me inside he slams the door shut and flips the lock. "On second thought, I *am* in the mood for your mouth."

He slams me up against the wall, grabs the front of my pants, and drops his mouth to suck on my throat.

The change of direction almost gives me whiplash.

Still, my body responds without fail. When your mate calls you out for some sexual healing, you do your best to comply. My blood rushes south. My cock hardens. And my drunken buzz takes me on a trippy ride.

"I need you, Rhy." He runs an explorative hand under my jacket and across the plains of my chest. The heat of his touch is searing, and I swallow as it moves lower.

"But not here," I say, kicking myself for shining a light of sanity on this moment. "You haven't claimed me in public. As far as the quadrant knows, you're happily mated to Keyla and Dillan."

He winces. "Don't say her name. I can't... this isn't about her. It's about you and me."

If only that were true.

He pegs me with a look that's so anguished and lost it kills my resolve to resist. "I need you, Rhy. You and me... uncomplicated... working off the brutality of life like before. Please."

How do I say no to that? He needs *me*. I'm the only one he wants at this moment. I meet him nose-to-nose and a rush of his desire hits me.

Damn, he smells good.

Easing him a half-step back, I soak in his beauty and my cock makes a solid attempt to break free from my jeans. Creed can be elegant and regal, but there's also another side to him that is raw and primal.

That's who's looking at me now.

I try to focus my drunken mind to assess the situation. The bathroom is a five-by-five box, somewhat clean, and private enough that we can take a moment to polish the countertop. I'm sure we're not the first two people to ejaculate in here.

He needs this. My dragon and I need it too.

"And then we go home," I say. "Without argument."

He dips his chin. "Whatever you say."

Like I believe that. I shrug off my jacket and hang it and my shoulder harness on the door handle. While I'm doing that, Creed's fine, loose slacks drop to the floor. He steps free of them and looks me over like he's about to devour me.

"You're sure you want to do this here?"

"Don't I look sure?" He stalks forward, his cock hard and thick, and pointed straight at me. "I need what only you and I have. You aren't afraid of my anger. You know how to defuse me and make the hurting stop."

It's true. I know what he needs and I'm up for the punishment.

After unbuckling my weapons belt, I push my pants and boxers down my thighs and let them pool around my ankles. Then, I lean back against the counter of the sink and grin as Creed's gaze locks on.

With strong, sure strokes I grab my cock and prime myself, running my grip from base to tip and then back down again. "We've got no liquid glide here, so we'll have to self-lubricate."

He licks his lips and another rush of that heady spice of his fills the air. "I'll help."

Bending at the waist, he lowers himself before me and sucks my erection between his lips. My hips buck, the heat of his mouth sending a bolt of sensation straight to my balls. "Yeah. That helps. That's good... so good."

I lace my fingers into the fall of his long, silver hair, and pull him against my hips. My cock pulses as he takes me in fully. I close my eyes and the room spins in a chaotic swirl, so I open them up again.

Okay, I've got too much of a buzz going to close my eyes. Lesson learned.

Heat blooms at the base of my sac as the pressure of release starts to build. "Damn, you're a beast tonight."

"I need inside you before I lose my mind."

Straightening, he pushes up against my side, gripping me hard. My breath escapes in a wild rush as he starts a rough rub and tug.

We've played this game many times and my dragon paces within, knowing what comes next. Creed and I are both dominant males, but when we come together, one of us has to take the punishment for the other one to give it.

There's never been any confusion about how those lines are drawn.

Creed fucks me... and I love it.

I growl as the *tick-tick-tick* of precum counts off his strokes. With every pounding glide up and down my shaft, the tension burns hotter.

"Yes," I growl, my chest pumping as my balls burn with the need to release. "Don't stop. Pump my cock."

He does. With a fierceness that speaks of how desperate he is, he pumps his hand, squeezing with such a delicious grip that I spill the slick cream he's after.

I close my eyes and ride out the convulsions of my release. Breathing heavily, the drugging scent of his need and anticipation fills my senses.

Creed is addictive.

He spins me around without fanfare. One moment I'm enjoying the sensations of shattering and the next I'm bent at the waist and pinned on the countertop beside the sink.

A rough hand between my shoulder blades holds me in place

as the cum he primed from me is put to use. He swipes warm moisture against my ass and then slicks over the head of his cock.

Watching him in the mirror is a rare gift.

I revel in the focus in his expression. Heated desire lights up his dark, haunted gaze as he grinds his cock against my ass. The blunt head of his crown presses at my opening.

He's so slecking beautiful.

"Brace yourself."

I always do. My blood roars.

I love our dark and dirty moments.

The penetration is hard and very deep. It stings at first—it always does. Creed's a big boy and without proper lubrication, sex with him is that much more invasive. Still, it's amazing.

The crown breaching is my favorite part.

There's an erotic moment at the entry point when his cock demands to be accepted. It's both mindless pleasure and breathless anticipation at once.

And then he breaches.

Sensation explodes up my spine and I groan and arch back into the cradle of his hips. He hesitates, for half a beat while our bodies absorb and settle. That one moment of relative calm is all I get before the storm.

He starts a deep in and out, and I push up onto my elbows to leverage his thrusts. Greedy fingers grip my hips as his strength comes into play. The intensity of the ride gears up quickly from hunger to pounding into me with almost violent force.

Creed is carnal impulse... I'm his willing vessel.

He's out of his head and that's the entire point. For this moment, there is only him and me and the sound of flesh meeting flesh and the smell of his need and my mating scent pouring out of my skin.

We are frenzy.

We are racing hearts and throbbing need.

Bracing my palms on the backsplash of the sink, I watch our joining in the reflection of the mirror. He's close. Over the past two years, I've memorized every expression, breath, and sound he makes.

His orgasm is burning, aching to gain freedom.

"Do it... fill me."

He grimaces, his breath coming in panting gasps. "Fuck you feel good." He shoves a hand under my chest and locks a hold onto my shoulder.

With the leveraged grip, he pistons even harder.

I use all of my dragon strength to keep from getting driven head-first into the mirror above the sink. The muscles in my left arm burn with the exertion as I shift my right arm between my thighs.

Gripping my shaft, I orgasm instantly.

I thrust my hips forward, tossing and coming in hot spurts down the front of the counter. Maybe I should care about the mess, but I don't.

I don't give a shit where my cum ends up.

Creed curses behind me and the release he pumps into me is soul-shattering for both of us.

Panting hard, I bring my arm back up to the countertop to steady my balance and to avoid buckling to the floor. "Shit, Creed. That was next level," I pant, my drunken buzz and loss of fluids making my head spin. "Did you manage to clear your head? Creed?"

He meets my gaze briefly, his gaze unfocused... and then his eyes roll back, and he drops like a rock.

"Slecking hell."

Keyla

By the time we wrap up with the officers and get back to the castle, it's close to the dinner hour. Doc's stomach is growling so loudly he's drawing attention as we exit the shuttle bus and head for the entrance. I laugh and pat the rock-hard ridges of his belly. "I should pack snacks for you as they do for Calli now that she's pregnant."

Doc grins. "Sorry. Not much I can do about it. I ate what Creed made for me this morning, but I don't think he's got a handle on how to feed a bear wildling yet."

"I don't suppose it's that different from a dragon."

"You're likely right, but I'm not sure he and Rhy were sharing breakfast. From what Rhy mentioned it was more an after-dark workout between them and then he slipped back to his room."

It hurts a little that Rhylan didn't get cast off with guilt and anger as I did, but I try not to look too closely at it. Grief is tricky.

"Majesty." Two castle guards open the door for us.

"Thank you, gentlemen." I offer each of them a smile and continue deeper into the castle proper. "I think it's best if we go back with Kotah to handle the Raven situation at the palace. It'll give Creed a moment to be alone with his grief and maybe sort out a few things."

"Do you think it's wise to pull back? He snubbed us, but that was a knee-jerk reaction to finding a female he loved tortured and breathing her last breath."

The horror of that makes it difficult to pull oxygen into my lungs. The pressure in my chest feels like someone has parked one of Hawk's SUVs on my sternum and refuses to back it off.

"I'm not giving up or running away. I'm simply giving him a day or two to confront his feelings without our presence complicating things. I have things to deal with and so does he."

When we arrive at the doors leading to the royal residences, two more guards open things up to let us pass. "Majesty."

"Thank you, gentlemen."

Our suite is quickly becoming home to me and even more so because when we step into the living room, Kotah, Jaxx, and Hawk are lounging on the couches, chatting and sharing a drink.

The three of them stand as I enter, and I chuckle. "I'm your sister-in-law, not your princess. You don't need to be so formal."

"A princess in one realm, a queen in another," Jaxx says, holding up his glass. "Seems to me we should not only stand but also bow."

I snort. "Please don't. If you want to do something for me, you can make me a drink."

"Coming up," Jaxx says, heading over to the bar.

Kotah's gaze narrows as he studies me. "What happened? It didn't go well for you in Clarinta?"

I draw a deep breath and smile at Doc. "Would you mind asking Calli to join us, so I only have to tell the story once?"

While he does that, I accept the tumbler from Jaxx and swallow some of the haze and grapefruit juice concoction he's been working on. "That's good. Thanks."

Calli and Dillan come back into the living room, and I tell them about how our morning circled the drain.

"And the witch had her all this time?" Calli says.

Doc nods. "She was sucking her dry of life force. Lukas said the power Bloom would've given her was both physical and magical."

"That's appalling," Hawk says. "I can't imagine the suffering the poor girl endured."

"And now Creed is flaying himself for being happy and in love with you while she suffered," Calli says.

I nod. "Which is why I've decided now is the time to deal with the treachery of our own realm."

Kotah shakes his head. "What do you mean? What treachery?"

Hawk steps to the side and I join my brother on the sofa. Pulling him down to sit with me, I shift on the cushion to face him. Squeezing his hands, I meet his troubled gaze. "When we were in the Travon badlands the other day, Rhylan told me what he knew about Laryssa and Sebastian's plot to take control of our realm."

His gaze narrows. "More than her trying to seize us by force when the portal gate opened?"

"Yes. For the past few years, Sebastian had someone on the palace staff poisoning Father. Adahy was right. Raven is no friend to our realm."

Kotah rubs a rough hand over his mouth and sighs. "So, weaken the realm by killing off the Fae Prime and then kill me at the coronation to seize control."

"That was their fallback objective, yes, but originally, they intended to put you into office assuming your age and indifference to ruling would make you weak in the eyes of the realm. Sebastian planned on offering them a strong leader."

I squeeze his hands, waiting for the hurt and self-recrimination to come.

Only it doesn't.

"Are you all right?" I cant my head to the side, assessing his scent and physical cues.

"Of course. Why wouldn't I be?"

Hawk shifts to sit on the stone coffee table and sets his glass down. "Keyla told me about this last night, worried you might feel in some way responsible for your father's death or hurt to be so underestimated."

Kotah returns his gaze to me, and his surprise is genuine. "Sister mine, I have run through every possible scenario for how and why I ended up as Fae Prime. I realized months ago that if Father was being poisoned as Adahy claimed that inserting a weak and unprepared leader was the objective."

"You did?"

"Of course. Why do you think I've spent so much energy transforming into the leader our world needs? It certainly isn't because I want it or because Father passed and it's my duty. I did it because the fae citizens of our realm deserve to live in peace with a strong leader who cares for them. It's the only reason I took the throne."

"So, people like my father couldn't," Hawk says, the scent of his pride strong in the air.

"You never cease to amaze us, Wolf," Jaxx says, raising his tumbler.

Calli looks at me and rolls her eyes. "Why do we worry so much about them?"

"Apparently for no reason at all." I let out a long breath and lean forward to hug my brother. "I'm so relieved. I didn't want this to hurt you."

"There is nothing anybody outside our family can do to hurt me, Keyla. As long as my mates and you and yours are well—*all* is well."

Calli winks at me from over Kotah's shoulder. "Does this mean we're headed back to the palace to kick Raven's ass?"

"Hells yeah, it does," Jaxx says. "About time too. I bet she thinks she got away with it."

Hawk nods. "The moment we get back through the portal gate, I'll find out what my people have learned. If she thought herself in the clear, maybe she let her guard down. Maybe something she did will lead us to my double-crossing half-brother."

"Damn," Calli says. "If we get Raven *and* Hunter in the same takedown that would be doubly sweet."

Jaxx nods. "When do we leave?"

Cue all eyes turning to me. "When Lukas and Brant get back. If Creed hasn't returned from delivering Bloom's body to her family, I'll leave him a note."

"A detailed, kind note," Kotah says, warily.

"Yes, brother mine. I'm not angry or burning any bridges, I simply believe he needs some solitude to sort through things. I would. And since we're mirrored souls, I'm guessing he feels the same way."

CHAPTER EIGHT

Creed

a cool breeze blows at me, tickling my face with my hair. It's incessant. Annoying. I want it to stop. I just can't seem to lift my arm at the moment to wipe my hair out of my face. What. The. Fuck.

It takes a few tries, but after a long while, I manage to pry one eye open wide enough to take in the scenery.

Stars. Outdoor furniture. A mountainous, scaled form curled up next to me. Huh. It's not every day you wake up next to a sleeping dragon.

I roll my gaze toward the two-mooned sky above and correct my thought. It's not every *night* you wake up next to a sleeping dragon.

As my mind fog clears, the pieces start to fall into place. We're on my parent's private verandah atop the king's tower of Thornebane Castle.

Rhy must've flown us home before he passed out. Smart male that Rhylan. He opted to land here where no one would see us rather than go through the corridors of the castle with a very drunk king.

Fuck, lying on the stone patio is bruising my ass. I'm uncoordinated as I roll to my side and push up to my knees. Shit, I'm still really fucking drunk.

I need to—*whoa.*

With rubber legs and the world spinning, I won't make it back to my suite. I rest a moment and rethink the idea of relocation. My head lolls to the side and I eye the outdoor couch.

Now that I could probably manage.

"I'm polluted," Rhylan mumbles into the stone of the verandah floor.

I glance back and he's no longer a dragon. He's a naked heap of a man. "You and me both. How did we get here? The last thing I remember is us fucking in that washroom."

Rhylan musters some strength and rolls onto his back. He stares bleary-eyed up at the two moons and rubs his hair out of his face with sloppy hands. "I'm not surprised that's where your memories crash to a halt. You climaxed like a beast and then immediately proceeded to pass out. Do you know how hard it is to dress a guy when he's out cold and you're drunk as shit? I deserve a slecking medal."

I try to remember but I've got nothing. Nothing except being bombarded by my failures. Nothing but drowning in grief and regret when I realized that husk of a female was my beautiful Bloom.

"Shit, this hurts, Rhy. It feels like Laryssa cracked me open from beyond the grave and ripped my heart from my chest."

"I'm not in much better shape. Only it was Shadowcaster and my slecking twin who hollowed me out. You know that disc you asked me about earlier?"

"Yeah."

"It's an exile disc. It means I'm no longer considered a dragon of honor. I've been excommunicated from my brood. *Annnd* to cut the wound deeper, Vikarus volunteered to serve it to me. He slecking volunteered! He wanted to be the one to wreck me."

Fuck that's cold. "I'm sorry, Rhy. I never meant for us to cost you—well, everything."

We lay there in silence for a bit before the collision of my two worlds starts to invade. Pain oozes from my chest like I've been stabbed and am bleeding out. On a reflex, I move a sloppy hand over my chest to make sure I'm not covered in leaking plasma.

Nope. It's all a cruel illusion.

"Rhy?"

"Yeah."

"Do you think she'll forgive me?"

"Which *she* are you asking about, Bloom or Keyla?"

Motherfucker, why not twist the knife? "I meant Keyla, but you're right... I failed them both."

"You didn't fail either of them. There was no way for you to know the Blood Witch had Bloom and no way to help her if you had. And as for Keyla... she loves you and is committed. She'll forgive you for a moment of madness. If she's truly your mirrored-self, she should know exactly where you're coming from."

Good. That's good. I fist my hand and hold it in the air for a symbolic bump.

Rhylan crawls across the stone and drops back down next to my head. "As soon as you can stand upright, I'll get you back to your suite and you can apologize. It'll be fine. I promise."

With Rhy's reassurance in the air, I give up my effort to get to the couch and decide to sleep it off a bit more before confronting my mistakes. I close my eyes and reach out on our private channel.

I'm sorry, Little Wolf. Please forgive me.

The King's Tower isn't far from the suite where Honor and I live. She should've heard me.

Maybe I'm too drunk...

Or she's too angry to respond.

Fuck. I wish I was sober enough to get her... to make her understand....

Doc

The eight of us are through the portal gate and back in our realm before dark on the human side of the portal. Keyla's putting up a solid front, but it's just that—she's fronting. Still, with everything that happened so fast with Creed, stepping back and touching base with our lives before isn't a bad idea.

"Hello, Pennsylvania," Calli says, waving to the FCO crew as we emerge into the clearing on the earth side of the portal rift. "Hello, Mallory."

The hulderfolk male Hawk brought from the FCO Manhattan office grins from ear to ear. He stands and rounds his desk opposite the gate exit, his tail swishing behind him as he rushes to greet us. "Welcome home, sirs and ma'ams. I do hope your trip to StoneHaven went well. Is everyone well?"

"Very well," Hawk says, extending a hand to the guy. "But, I admit, it's good to be back. I see things are advancing nicely with the portal hub."

They are. When Creed and I passed through the rift a week ago, the energy was simply a power rift in the open air. Now the gate opens up into a thirty by fifty foot atrium with a station for the portal controls and an office area for Mallory, our realm security officer.

"This place looks amazing," Calli says smiling up at the ceiling high above. "How did you get a building in place already?"

Mallory grins. "It's modular. Mr. Barron told me to spare no expense and get this end of the gate up and running. My wife has a talent for spending other people's money. She is in her happy place, putting together a welcoming yet impressive hub. I hope it meets your expectations, sir."

Hawk smiles, taking in the atrium. "Add a couple of reinforced, security-grade skylights and it's perfect. You've done well, my friend. Thank your wife for me and tell her to keep up the great work."

~

Keyla

The eight of us make the short walk through the forest and over the newly constructed bridge leading us to the other side of the river. All this land belongs to the corporation of the Fae Concealment Office, which is to say, Hawk. The Pixie Queen may have tried to assume ownership of the part where the portal gate is, but my brother and his mates figured that out quickly enough and put a stop to her claims.

"You okay, girlfriend?" Calli asks.

We're standing at the edge of the tree line waiting for Hawk's helicopter pilot to finish with his ground checklist. The guys are busy being guys and chatting about guy things and that leaves me and Calli alone for some much-needed girl talk.

"It's good to be home—don't get me wrong—but somehow it doesn't feel right."

"What doesn't? Being here or leaving Creed and Rhylan back in Dornte?"

I think about that and answer as honestly as I can. "In my mind, I realize that less than two weeks have passed since Creed and I kicked off the whole chaotic adventure but in my heart and soul it feels like much longer. We've been building a life in a different world and I'm no longer in sync with what my life was here."

Calli hooks her arm through mine, linking our elbows. "I know exactly how that feels. After Hawk arranged for us to take down Sonny and his gang of drow assholes, he took me back to my apartment in California. I needed to settle up with my landlord and pack up a few things I didn't want to lose."

"And what happened?"

"It was weird. I felt like a stranger in my own life. The apartment didn't feel the same. My things didn't hold the same interest. It was like you said, I was out of sync with my own life."

"Did it go away?"

She shrugs. "I don't know. I asked Hawk to have my things packed for storage and I never went back. The important part is that my life with them felt right and real. I focused on that and then my old life stopped mattering."

"I get that—I do—it's just impossible for me to focus on my new life right now."

Calli offers me a sad smile. "He'll be all right. Guys need a minute to sort through emotions. He already came to terms with Bloom's death. To find out she was not only alive but in the hands of his enemies is a huge blow to his pride, both as a man and a protector. He feels like he failed her, and his first instinct was to condemn himself for the happiness he found with you."

I sigh. "I understand all that and all I want is the chance to help him through it. I feel his pain and it hurts me that he's hurting."

"Rhylan's there with him. They'll figure it out until you get back to him."

I look at the helicopter and sigh. "It would be handy if we didn't have to fly back to Kansas every time something happened. I realize you guys belong here now and Doc and I belong there, but I liked it in the palace and the castle when you were right across the hall."

"Me too. Your brother's struggling with that as well. He knows he needs to be here, but he wants to be close to you to be available if you need him."

I squeeze her arm against my side and sigh. "Looks like the universe has a different plan."

"But we'll see you all the time when this baby arrives." She rubs her hand over the bump on her belly. "I never wanted kids, never was around kids, and have no idea what to do with a kid. I'm so lost about what to expect it's crazy."

I chuckle. "Well, if you need a break, I'm happy to step in and help. Although, knowing how excited your guys are, I doubt I'll get much time to play Aunt Keyla."

~

Creed

I wake mid-afternoon with my head fuzzy and my stomach churning with eminent upheaval. "Ah, fuck." Rolling off my parent's bed, I work fast to orient myself and make it into the bathroom before my night's poor choices rise in revolt.

My knees throb from crashing into the marble tiles but that doesn't hurt half as much as the loss and regret I'm still drowning in.

After another couple of rounds of up and out, I groan and rest my head on the cool tiles. My memories drift back to the last time I was in this bathroom. Ironically, I was puking then too.

I was twelve... maybe thirteen and I'd attended my first heir's event. Satune, the Prince of Travon, got hold of a bottle of haze from the party and challenged me to meet him shot for shot.

I did... until I couldn't see straight.

Father brought me in here and gave me a lecture. *It takes a strong man to rise to a challenge. It takes a stronger man to walk away from one.*

My father was a great and wise man.

Big shoes to fill.

I look at myself lying half-dead on his bathroom floor and wince. "All hail, the King of Dornte."

Closing my eyes, I let that sink in. I am a king now. I addressed the citizens less than forty-eight hours ago promising them I would be the leader they need.

I doubt very much they need a drunk asshole puking and fucking up his mating.

As much as I loved Bloom—and I did—I was a posh prince and life was enchanted. I wasn't the man I am now or that I need to be going forward.

If Laryssa was good for anything, it was how her actions against me, Honor, and my parents taught me the reality that life can be violent and cruel. She forced me to grow up and realize I'm not enchanted after all.

Bloom wasn't destined to be my forever love.

Keyla is.

And what I feel for my Little Wolf is... I can't even put it into context. It's just—more.

That's part of the reason I'm buried by guilt. It's more than me moving on while Bloom suffered. It's me seeing my future in Keyla.

With that revelation in mind, I get my ass off the bathroom floor and rinse my mouth and hands at the sink. After patting my face dry, I check myself in the mirror. Not very regal. "I look like I had an all-nighter and slept in my clothes."

Which, of course, I did.

Shuffling back out to the bedroom, I take in my parents' chambers—the royal suite.

Laryssa's things are polluting the space and it offends everything in me. When my parents lived in these rooms, the space was decorated in gold and black. It was elegant and sophisticated.

Laryssa changed the décor.

She made herself right at home and it sickens me.

I can't begin to process that with everything else I'm dealing with, so I take a look around for Rhylan and when I'm sure he's not here, I tuck and straighten as much as I can and head back to my suite.

I practice my apology all the way up the hall, thankful I don't run into anyone. I'll get this off my chest, shower, brush my teeth, and when my stomach settles, I'll make love to her and show her how very much she means to me.

When I get to our suite, I press my hand on the security screen and unlock things.

"Keyla? Are you here, Little Wolf?" Closing the door behind me, I scan the entire apartment for her mental signature.

Nothing.

Maybe... I cross the hall and knock on the door to the Auburn Suite. "Kotah? Calli? Anyone here?"

When no one answers, I let myself inside and my heart sinks. Their things are gone.

Heart hammering triple time I race back to our suite and run full tilt to my closet. Rounding the corner, I stop dead and groan. Keyla and Dillan's duffle bag is gone.

"Fuck me," I hiss, frantically searching the space for something to grab hold of. "Nononono."

I'm about to go into a full spiraling tailspin when I see the folded note propped against the center pillow on the bed. My feet pound against the floor as I close the distance and launch onto the mattress.

I run a trembling finger over her writing.

Creed

Thumbing the paper open, I'm terrified to read her words. I'm also terrified not to.

Before you panic, I'm gone but I'm not leaving you.
  I love you. You are my mirrored soul, remember?
  How could you think I'd walk away from that?

I bark a laugh and swipe a hand under my eyes to clear my vision. Closing my eyes, I take a couple of deep breaths and try to restart my heart. "Sorry, I panicked."

Take the day or two that we're gone to sort through your regrets and your guilt. You loved Bloom and she deserved better. I understand that. I also know your heart. We're fine. Yes, I'm hurt, but nothing was done that can't be healed with you snuggling and spoiling me a little in my grotto.

I chuckle. "I like the way you think, Little Wolf."

Don't start the interviews without me. I want to be at your side for all the King of Dornte stuff. I'm all-in. We're going to rock this quadrant together. But before I can focus on Dornte, I need to be with Kotah to confront Raven and help Mother understand what happened to Father.

Know that my heart is with you, and I miss you already. I love you more with every breath,

Evermore, your Little Wolf.

I swipe my sleeve across my eyes and draw a deep steadying breath. To reassure myself, I read her words over twice more to ensure there is no subtext or hidden meaning I've missed.

Of course, there's not. Keyla doesn't do subtext.

Nakeyla Northwood is the most honest and frank female I've

ever had the pleasure of knowing. If she needs you to know something, she speaks her truth, and you understand without guessing.

I love you more with every breath,
  Evermore, your Little Wolf.

With my heart patched together, I set the note where she left it and head into the bathroom.

It's time for me to grab the reins of this quadrant and start being the king my people need.

The king my *mates* need as well.

CHAPTER NINE

Rhylan

*T*he heat of morning sun sizzles the scales of my wings as I close the distance between me, my humiliation, and likely my destruction. Exile is a no-go in the realm of dragons. Returning to confront my brood is not only stupid, it's punishable by death.

Still, here I am.

If all goes well, I won't be confronting anyone. All I want to do is speak to my mom and ask her about something the Blood Witch said. *The only way to truly rise to the top is to risk more than others believe is safe.*

I've heard Shadowcaster say it more than once. A coincidence? Maybe, but I don't think so.

Shadowcaster was in league with Laryssa and it's reasonable that he might be in league with the witch too. If that's the case, my mother being tethered to the man's side can be used to my advantage.

Maybe I can find out more about where she frequents and who else might know where she is.

Knowing my brood and how hard they party after dark on a week's end, I'm betting most of them are as hungover and out cold as Creed is right now. If the universe is on my side, I'll be able to sneak in, speak to my mother, and get out before anyone even knows I'm here.

My dragon growls. *Since when has the universe ever been on our side?*

Good point. But hey, Keyla and Creed can't be the only two in the grand design of change, can they? I'm worth a little fae magical intervention.

As I reach the jagged peaks of the Travon Traverse, I throw up a glamor and hide my presence. Normally, I do this to protect the location of our brood lands. Today I do it to keep from being seen by my own people.

It's been two years since I've been home.

When Shadowcaster made his deal with Laryssa and sold us into servitude, we were sent off and quickly forgotten. The ill-begotten sons of a traitor.

Knowing that Vikarus ran back to that piece of shit when he found out about me and Creed is a shock.

Was my relationship with the prince a bigger betrayal than our brood alpha's claim on our mother and the murder of our father?

Even if Vikarus was furious with me, I can't reconcile him betraying me to Shadowcaster and mounting an attack at the compound.

If he wants to be enemies and draw a line between us, so be it. I am on the right side of things for the first time in forever and I don't regret the choices I made.

Still, I worry about the next battle.

At Laryssa's compound, my dragon brethren were unprepared for Calli. I have no illusions of grandeur. Calli and I holding them off during Honor's rescue was nothing other than them not knowing what to make of the Fae Phoenix and her powers.

That won't work in our favor again, but it did the job—Honor is safe, and I was able to give Creed back at least one of the women taken from his life.

Once I find the witch and Lukas unravels her curses, both Honor and Creed can finally be free of her and all the damage she and Laryssa caused.

I bank right as I drop beneath the first outpost marker and glance toward the sentry station. As I expected, the guard has his eyes closed and looks like he's sleeping off a rough night.

Perfect. If luck is on my side, I might get out of this without getting killed.

Yeah, except I've never been lucky in my life.

∾

Keyla

Kotah and I spend an hour with our mother, going over what we know and what we suspect in regard to our father's assassination. At first, she sits very still with her jaw locked and her gaze hard.

In the world of Malayna Northwood, this means she doesn't believe us. Eventually, after Kotah finishes going over the events, Hawk hands her a file.

"When Keyla told me what she learned three days ago, I tasked a team to dig up every secret Raven has pushed under the rug. I wanted to know what drug was used, where she got it, who else knew about it, and how she was connected to my father. Also, in all the years she was here, was she communicating with my father or my brother or some other intermediary."

Mother's lips are pursed into a fine line. "How could you

possibly be certain of these things now? My husband was burnt on a pyre. Surely if Raven was as devious as Nakeyla says, she's also clever enough not to have damning evidence lying around for your spies to find."

Spies? Seriously?

"Mother, we understand it's hard to believe but Hawk has proven everything I was told."

"By a traitorous dragon," she snaps. "A male who betrays his queen has no honor and should be considered an unreliable disgrace."

The gasp of my breath is loud in the silence of the room. "Rhylan is a good man, Mother. He was in an impossible situation, and he chose to honor what is right over a duty foisted on him by a vindictive alpha."

"You are naïve, Nakeyla. Open your eyes."

I tap the folder Hawk gave her and get back to the point. "Yes, let's open our eyes. Raven fooled everyone, Mother. Hawk's team found the evidence to support Rhylan's claims. The royal lab preserved blood samples from every examination. They never found the problem because the poison used was undetectable unless they tested for it specifically."

"How convenient."

"Also, Hawk's men found and recorded calls to Raven's private phone that connect her with a courier, and that courier has been connected back to Sebastian's lab in Manhattan."

Mother lifts her chin, growing more defiant instead of less. "These things can be falsified, child. You don't spend as much time with lies and deception as I do without developing a sense of detection. I am a wildling wolf. Do you not think that in over a decade of service, I would've smelled her supposed ill intentions against your father?"

"No, you wouldn't. That beautiful ring she never takes off, the one I've commented on a dozen times, it's an heirloom to the

Fae Witch Botanda. It is an emotional glamor, so no, you wouldn't have smelled her ill intent."

"Nakeyla, enough. Your attack on my dearest ally is not only childish and petty, it's cruel. You should be ashamed of yourself. I taught you better."

I lift my hands and turn things over to Hawk. "I give up. Bring Raven in and maybe she'll believe us when she hears it from Raven herself."

It takes a few minutes for Hawk to get Lukas from the receiving parlor and to get a bespelled Raven settled on the sofa in front of us. Lukas assures us that with her ring removed and his truth spell, she is open to answer all of our questions.

He starts off the interrogation with a few easy questions about her name and where she lives and then moves into the more hard-hitting subjects of her deceit.

"And did you enter into your agreement with my father willingly or were you coerced?" Hawk asks.

The glint of pleasure that flashes in her eyes sends a chill down my spine. "More than willing. Everyone knows the Northwoods are a waste of leadership. Fae are more powerful, more magical, and more capable than humans, yet we're forced to hide in the shadows while the meek inherit the earth."

"And how did you enter into this bond with him? How did he recruit you to his cause?"

"Recruit me? He didn't need to recruit me. Our plans took shape across the table at family dinners."

"Family?" Hawk says, clearly confused. "How?"

"Hunter and I were married as teens. We've been planning the takeover of the realm with Sebastian for more than a decade."

Married?

Well, I guess that explains why she never dated.

Father and Mother often joked that she was too dedicated to

her work to go find someone. Apparently, we were right, except the work she was dedicated to was destabilizing the realm.

"I've heard enough," Mother says, rising from her seat. She straightens the fall of her skirt with stiff hands and lifts her chin. "I'm going to my private chambers, and I'd like you all to leave. Children, you will finish this and come speak to me in private."

With that, the former Fae Prima leaves the room.

Hawk looks even more confused. "I get that we're dismissed but did she believe us?"

I shrug. "Who knows. She is who she is, and no one will ever force her to believe anything she doesn't want to. The great Malayna Northwood knows all."

Kotah stands and gestures toward the door. "We've done what we can."

"What will be done with her?" I ask, taking a hard look at the woman I considered a friend and confidant.

"She's earned herself a life in confinement," Hawk says, standing to walk us out. "We'll take her to an FCO facility and ensure she never acts against you or your family again."

Kotah pats Hawk's shoulder and nods. "Get her out of the palace as quickly as you can. Her presence here is an offense to our family."

"Understood." Hawk's gaze locks with my brother and by the soft smile that appears I know they're having a private conversation. There's no missing the love the five of them share and I'm so thankful.

There's no way I could live in another realm thinking Kotah was taking on the world alone like he always has. To know that four other people cherish him—and honestly, I'll add in Jaxx's parents and sister too—paves the way for me to strike off and explore my destiny.

I smile at Doc, standing at attention beside the doorway. His arms are clasped at his back, his muscled chest fighting the constraints of his gray top.

I love you. I say across our private channel.

Right back attcha, babe. He opens the door for Hawk and Lukas to exit with Raven and then closes us in once more. *Is it inappropriate to say your ass is looking fine in those slacks?*

I stifle a laugh. *Not as inappropriate as this.*

I project images of him wrapping his arms around me and carrying me into the art alcove on our right. With rough hands, he fumbles with the clasp of my pants and pushes them down my silky thighs. His cock springs free and when he presses forward, I wrap my legs around his hips and sink over his heated shaft.

The soft rumble of his bear triggers a release of moisture and my inner muscles throb.

Fuck. You're killing me.

The moment Mother is settled...

Ready when you are.

~

"Are they gone?" Mother emerges from her chambers, her disposition as dour and hard as it was only moments ago when she retreated.

"They are," Kotah says.

"Good. Walk with me. I wish to stretch my legs."

"Of course, Mother." Kotah and I fall into step and join her as she strides for the door.

Doc opens the door for us and dips his chin. "Majesty." He winks as I pass. "My Queen."

I chuckle and give him a quick brush of my lips.

Mother looks over at me and frowns. "We are not animals, Nakeyla. As a queen of a realm, you must hold yourself to a higher standard. Surely, you can get through a few hours without being indecent."

I roll my eyes. "It was a tasteful kiss within our private

rooms. No one saw. And for your information, wildlings actually *are* animals, Mother."

"But you need not act like an animal needing to rut your bear."

My wolf paces to the fore as Doc's tension rises behind me. "I don't consider having a healthy sexual appetite for my mate to be rutting. That's rude. You're being intentionally crass."

"What is crass is you taking two men into your mating bed. I thought you to have more sense."

I chuff. "You're out of the mating loop, Mother. It's three now. Dillan, Creed, and Rhylan."

"Rhylan? The hoodlum dragon? Powers save me, daughter, that male came into our lives with hostility and attacked us. Then he betrayed his duties and allowed his queen to be overthrown."

"First of all, he didn't attack us. He was ordered to enter the realm with a show of strength. Rhylan is a soldier. He followed Laryssa's orders. And considering his decision to overthrow Laryssa was made to save my life, Kotah's, and all our mates, I would think you'd be a little more forgiving of the optics."

Her disapproval doesn't cut me as deep as it has in the past. In fact, it annoys me more than anything. "I don't smell the dragon's scent in your mating bond."

"We haven't gotten that far yet."

"Thank the Powers. Then there is time to rethink and salvage some of your dignity."

I offer her a patient yet firm smile. "No, Mother. There is no rethinking needed. Rhylan is part of our pairing. We four are mates."

She makes a tsking sound I'm all too familiar with and turns to glare at my brother. "This is your fault."

Kotah arches a brow, looking amused. "Oh? And how is that, exactly?"

"If you showed restraint and chose a traditional mating, your sister wouldn't have gotten the idea to open her bed to every male who looked her way."

A deep growl rumbles from behind us.

Kotah's amusement fades and I shake my head. "It's fine boys. I don't need defending on this. I'm proud of my mates and of the bonds we've been forming. Mother is understandably upset. This is about her feeling betrayed and grieving for Father. I won't allow her to coax me into an argument."

We turn the corner toward the royal residence and pass the guards on the wide staircase. The moment I spot the blonde couple waiting on the first landing, my day brightens.

The Stantons.

Mother flicks her hand as she walks past Jaxx's parents. "Consider them yours. They ceased being my children long ago."

John and Maggie look startled by Mother's remarks, but Kotah and I wave away her concern. "Ignore her, Mama," Kotah says, hugging first Jaxx's mom and then his dad. "She is who she is and nothing and no one will change her."

Our parents were never huggers.

That's one of the best things about the Stantons adopting us as their pseudo kids—endless affection and support.

"We're so sorry to hear about your father, kids," Mama says taking one of our hands in each of hers. "Jaxx caught us up and we're heartbroken over the entire situation."

"Thank you." I squeeze Mama and then enjoy the heartfelt warmth of John's embrace. "It'll be hard for Mother, but honestly, it doesn't change much for us. Kotah and I came to terms with losing him."

"Come," Mama says, directing us across the landing. "I've got lunch ready in the suite and we're dying to hear all about your latest adventures."

I slide my arm around Mama's hip and the five of us head back to Kotah's residence.

~

Creed

I take the day to sober up and sit at Honor's bedside. It's surreal to see her lying in her bed. I can't count how many times I sat in here over the past two years, talking to the walls and trying to figure out how I was ever going to get her back. My mind would spin in endless circles, imagining all the ways I could make it happen.

I never once imagined Keyla and the Phoenix Quint.

She looks like she's sleeping but her mental energy says differently. I hate that even after finding her and freeing her, she's still trapped in the prison of Laryssa and the Blood Witch's making.

"We'll figure it out." I squeeze her foot beneath the covers. "Lukas is a talented guy and Keyla believes in him. He belongs to some high-powered Guild of Mages in the Human Realm. They all seem genuinely confident he'll figure out how to break that bitch's hold on us."

A knock on the outer door forces me off my ass.

I push to my feet, shut Honor's door, and cross our apartment into the living room. "Come."

The door opens and my mother's aide, Isabo, steps inside. The layers of her skirting swish with each step and I'm reminded of how Honor and I used to hear that sound and have enough time to stop messing around and straighten ourselves to appear the proper children we were expected to be.

She has aged in the passing years but remains as elegant and well-kept as ever.

Isabo folds her gloved hands against her front and lowers herself in a slight bow. "King Creed. I wondered if I might be of service to your mate. I realize I have been absent from the castle these past years, but after what happened. I, uh, couldn't face seeing that woman here. I abandoned you and your sister when I should've tried to be of aid."

I shake my head and gesture toward the sofas. "Did you attend my address in the Great Hall two nights ago?"

"No. I'm sorry. I was not."

We sit opposite one another, and I lay my arm along the back of the sofa. "I stated that all those loyal to my family have my complete understanding and pardon for anything that transpired since Laryssa's arrival. The woman was a parasite with no regard for lives or loyalties. That you are here now, and after all the years of devotion you showed my mother, of course, you're welcome back as the Queen's Aide—on one condition."

Isabo lifts her chin. "Sire? What condition is that?"

"Are you aware that the universe set things in motion with Keyla and her mate Dillan, so there are more than two in my mating?"

She straightens. "I saw your announcement last week where you said as much, yes."

"In truth, I was also in a relationship at the time of our soul-searing. Keyla encouraged me to invite my lover to join us, so there are four of us in this marriage."

Her eyebrows arch and disappear under her mauve bangs. I let her have a moment for that to sink in. "I understand it's unusual in this realm and I don't want you to take on something you're uncomfortable with."

"If I might ask, Majesty, how will that work?"

"Excuse me?" I peg her with a look.

Her hands come up as her cheeks flush bright pink. "Forgive me. No. I meant in a ruling sense. Your private affairs are, of course, your own. I meant how will the ruling of the quadrant be broken up? I am accustomed to being the Queen's Aide."

Oh, good. I wasn't about to get into my sex life with this woman. "Keyla and I will be the traditional ruling couple. You will aid her as you did my mother. She is royalty in her realm, so she is aware of her duties and responsibilities to our citizens. I simply mentioned our mating situation because Dillan and Rhylan must also be honored as our mates. If you hold issue with that, I'd rather know now."

She exhales heavily and her shoulders relax. "Then all is well. You will be a great King, Master Creed. Your situation is uncommon, yes, but not so different from the Phoenix and her Guardians. If the powers of the fae universe willed it so, who am I to have an opinion?"

I nod, thankful for her support. "Then I will introduce you to Keyla when she returns from her business in the Human Realm. If after meeting and talking, the two of you think yourselves a good fit, you may resume your duties at once."

"Wonderful," she says, folding her hands in her lap. "And until she returns, is there anything I can do to help you transition into your role?"

When I stand, she stands as well. "I'm glad you asked. I do have a project I would very much like for you to get started on right away. Could we begin right now?"

"Of course, Majesty. What can I do for you?"

CHAPTER TEN

Rhylan

*W*hen I land on the platform of the overlook, I listen for any sign of incoming hostilities. When nothing sparks my sense of survival, I shift back to two legs and step into the shadows.

If luck is on my side, Shadowcaster will be out flexing his muscles, bullying a weaker species of the fae, or unconscious with a bunch of naked whores.

That would leave my mother free to have a surprise visit from her exiled son.

The lair of my brood is found within a massive hollow in a mountain range along the north ridge of the Travon Traverse.

Other fae species know the general whereabouts of our home, but the entry point to the caverns is so deep within dragon territory no one has ever found it.

And likely never will.

The secrecy of its location is the number one tenet of our society. No one other than a dragon is permitted to know where our lair is located.

As a child, I thought that was paranoia. We are dragons. No one would dare act against us.

Then I grew up and began to interact with the outside world. I soon realized that as well as being recognized as the biggest and strongest of the wildling races, we are also known for being the least trustworthy and most despicable.

So much for the honor of the dragon clans.

The lair is made up of a massive open courtyard and then nine offshoot crevices that lead to a maze of caverns and pocketed stone caves. Clan Silverwing's cavern is down the left crevice and past the grotto pools. It was a glorious spot to grow up, rich with the heritage and honor of our clan.

It was the first thing Shadowcaster took from us after killing my father. Well, technically the second.

The first thing he took was our mother.

He stripped her Silverwing leathers from her body and forced her to submit to his advances while the entire brood watched on.

Our father's body wasn't even cold yet.

That was the foreshadowing of what our lives would be like from then on. Clan Silverwing went from being one of the most honored and revered ancient families of the dragon clans to the kin of the traitor who attacked the brood alpha.

Deep voices up ahead have me pressing tight to the jagged stone and dropping my gaze. When I come into view of the two males putting the moves on one of the ale girls from the pub, I pretend I'm checking something on my data tablet and keep walking.

The males are too busy focusing on the female to take note of me and the female wouldn't dare take her eyes off them for fear of losing any control she has.

In the years after our father's death, Vikarus and I grew highly skilled at navigating the lair unseen while in plain sight.

The key is to project an air of belonging—even when you don't.

The courtyard is fairly empty when I reach it. Two young boys on the far side of the open space are playing battle with wooden swords and cracking on one another.

There are also three women huddling close and whispering at the mouth of the fifth crevice.

"By all that's dark and destructive, what the slecking hell are you doing here?" The whispered hiss comes from my left as I'm yanked into what was once Silverwing domain. "What kind of shit for brains have you got guiding you these days?"

The smack to my ear rings in my head and I wince. "Mom. Take it easy. I came to check on you and explain what's been going on."

My mother is a weathered but beautiful blonde with a dagger-sharp tongue and a fist as hard as an anvil. She's tall and broad-shouldered and when she grabs a fistful of hair at my nape and drags me deeper into the passageways of my youth, there is nothing to be done but stumble along and follow.

When we're well away from the courtyard and beyond the distance that heightened hearing can pick up, mom turns and glares. "Did you stop using your thinking head when your cock head took over your life?"

I roll my eyes. "It's not like that. Creed got under my skin, but I never meant to mate him. My dragon saw him with his soul-seared lover, and I lost control."

"Lost your mind, you mean. Slecking hell, Rhylan. You're the smart one." She crosses her arms and leans in close. "Your brother has his strengths but he's not strategic like you. He doesn't see things the way you and I do. When he came back here and said you betrayed your duty and chose to lay with the prince, I didn't believe him. No way could my Rhylan be so slecking idiotic."

I sigh and throw up my hands. "Do I get a chance to tell you what happened? For sleck's sake, I am the strategic one, remember. Do you think I'd screw over this family on a whim?"

Mom lets out a suffering sigh. "I honestly don't know what to think. Go on then. Tell me your side."

So, I do.

I tell my mom about what Laryssa was like and how vile she was as a leader. I tell her about Creed and how I sympathized with him having his life and his heritage ripped from him for no other reason than a bitch's greed.

"But the universe bound Creed to Keyla and with Keyla came the Phoenix and her Guardians. The moment they were there to help Creed, him reclaiming his crown was set in motion."

She nods. "The soul-searing certainly suggests that you boys were on the wrong side of destiny."

"Exactly," I say, thankful that she gets it. "But even still, I would've served Laryssa to honor my oath."

"But then you mated the King? How? He was already mated."

"My dragon ascended and in a fit of fury, it just happened. And even after, I denounced it and kept up with my duties. I told Creed it was a mistake and he needed to move on with his mates and forget what happened."

"So, how did you get found out?"

"Laryssa had Creed's and the Phoenix Quint's apartments bugged. She must've heard talk because during a trip to Stone-Haven she asked for my weapon and her and her guards shot me three times at point-blank range."

Her eyes flare wide. "She meant to kill you? Without even speaking to you."

I nod. "I was in bad shape, but my new mates and the Phoenix Quint stepped in and rescued me. Dillan, our fourth, is a doctor and he patched me up using Calli's phoenix tears. Otherwise, I wouldn't have survived."

Mom frowns. "Duty is one thing, but I see the spot you were

in. You were bound to the wrong side of a losing battle, and you quite literally had to save your skin."

"Vikarus won't even hear me. It's like he doesn't know me. After all this time, he's treating me like I'm actually a traitor."

She waves that away. "Don't worry about your brother. I'll speak to him. He's always been too quick to act and too headstrong to see reason. He's your father's son to the bone and blood."

"And I'm yours."

She nods. "Gods help you, yes. All right. You've told me your tale of woe. Now tell me why you're really here."

Doc

It's late when Keyla and I leave the quint in their suite and wave goodnight to Jaxx's parents in the hall. I unlock the door and let Keyla into the room she and I shared secretly for weeks the last time we were here.

"Hello, old friend," I say, patting the bed. "We've missed you, haven't we, babe?"

Keyla chuckles, locking the door behind us and padding into the bathroom to get ready for bed. "Yes. We've also progressed quite a lot from the last time we were here. If I remember correctly, the last night we spent in that bed, I begged you to mate me, and you refused."

"That was when I was young and stupid."

She laughs. "That was two-and-a-half weeks ago."

"Okay, maybe just stupid."

The toilet flushes and the water runs for a bit. When she pads back into the room, she's as gloriously naked as ever. "So, tonight, when I beg you to pin me down and press inside me, what is the answer?"

"Yes, dear."

She smiles, struts around the end of the bed, and toys with her hardened nipples. "And when I say I need you to give me more, harder, rougher, what is the answer then?"

I pull my shirt off over my head and toe off my shoes. "Oh, yes, dear."

She giggles and climbs onto the mattress, prowling forward on her hands and knees. Her tits sway freely, the grace and beauty of her predator side stealing my sanity. "And if I tell you I want to orgasm and make love and fuck until we both pass out from exhaustion, what is the answer?"

My bear lets off a long growl as I yank my jeans open and shove them down my muscled thighs. "Yes, dear. Anything you say, dear. Absolutely anything."

"Good boy." She smiles up at me as she drops to the mattress and rolls onto her back. "Now, come here and get inside me."

I bite my bottom lip as I take in the beauty of her. Her chestnut hair is a scattered mess on the bed and invites me to rake my fingers through the silky lengths. Her cheeks are flushed, her lips glossy, and her eyes hold a brightness that speaks of how playful her wolf is tonight.

"Do you mind if I start with a hello to my girls?"

She giggles. "Who am I to tell you how to handle your business."

Yeah right. Keyla makes no secret when she wants something in bed. And now that I listen, things have gotten better and better.

Still, I want to start with a little worshipping of her body. Firm, round, and delicious. I draw my tongue over the budded tips of her breasts and my bear lets off a rumble of appreciation.

"Hello, ladies." Climbing over her to get into a better position, I take one of the mounds into my mouth and I play with the nipple of the other.

Damn.

Her skin tastes like the most succulent honey.

I swirl my tongue around her nipple and then blow on it. Keyla arcs off the mattress and presses further into my mouth.

"Like that, do you?"

"You know I do. You know what else I like?"

I chuckle, my bear letting off a deep sound of contentment. "Oh, I'm getting to that. I'm familiarizing myself first. So many things I want to touch and taste. Where's a male to begin?"

"Is that a rhetorical question or can I offer you a suggestion?"

I chuckle. "No need. I've been paying attention."

She smiles up at me. "And as much as I love foreplay—and I do—after the day we've had, I need you inside me—like, really soon. Or I might die."

"Well, what kind of a mate would I be if I let you die of wanton lust? That would be a complete waste of a great woman."

"Right? I think thoroughly sexing me up and many orgasms are the way to remedy that."

I am on board with that.

Climbing higher up her body, I claim her mouth, and the instant her hands stroke up and over my bare ribs, I'm lost in the moment, kissing her hard and sweeping my tongue into her mouth.

My fingers spear into her hair, and as I pull her deeper into my kiss, I send a prayer of thanks out to the fae universe that she is mine.

How did I hold back all those nights?

I have no clue.

With a long, hungry growl, I run my fingers across the entrance of her core and ensure she's ready for me.

Which is crazy because Keyla is always ready.

Warm, slick moisture coats my fingers and I brush over her clit and tickle through her folds.

Her body is so responsive.

She whimpers at the stroking, her back arching, her legs

falling wide to welcome me home. I lower my hips and replace my fingers with my cock and poise myself right where I need to be.

Slipping my damp fingers into my mouth, I swallow her essence. The taste of her nearly does me in.

"I could lose it, simply from the taste and scent of your honey, you know that?"

"I've heard how much bears love honey."

"It's true, we do."

"You know what I love?"

I chuckle. "Yes, dear."

I push back at the burning pressure tingling in my balls and focus on her. The steady thrum of her heart picks up speed as I brush her lips gently with mine.

I could kiss her for an eternity and never get enough.

Swaying my hips, I slick my crown in her heat. She groans, wrapping her legs around my hips, trying to force my entry. I chuckle at the impossibility of that.

She is a female wolf.

I am a male bear.

There's no forcing me into anything but I relent and give her what she wants. Thrusting forward, I sink into the depths of her and press her into the mattress. She stretches languidly beneath me, and I start a steady thrust and retreat.

"Yes, thank you."

I chuckle. Pleasuring Keyla comes as naturally as breathing. I know what she likes, I share her hunger, and I can read her body like she was made for me.

Because she was, my bear growls.

Yeah. She definitely was.

Circling my hips, I pick up the pace and build her toward her first orgasm of the night. Keyla likes to take the edge off hard and fast and then sink into a night of play. Who am I to argue with a girl with preferences?

Thrust and retreat. Thrust and retreat.

I close my eyes and let the sensation of gliding through her clenching muscles feed my soul. *This.* This is my happy place. This is where I want to be and what I want to be doing for the rest of time.

Joining with her is perfection. The building of her sexual tension. The scent of her pleasure filling the air. The feminine sounds she makes each time I sink fully inside her and trigger the clench of her greedy muscles.

Thrust and retreat. Harder. Faster.

Her nails dig into my shoulders and her hips begin to buck. I push her until she pants and writhes beneath me, penetrating her until our bodies slap together and I can't get any further inside her.

"Oh, yes..." she breathes. The first waves of orgasm hit and her muscles flex, gripping me with each heated stroke. "More."

"Yes, dear." Gone is my reserve to pamper my princess. I unhinge my hips and fill her with power-driven strokes. My abs and quads burn, my lungs fight for oxygen, my cells ignite with the amazing, sweaty friction of bodies fitting together as perfectly as we do.

Keyla cries out, her voice thready as her body shatters. She's a fit and powerful female and watching her swept away by her release is a beautiful thing. I smile, slowing things down while she rides out the first orgasm of the night.

When she catches her breath a little, I bend forward and claim her mouth. "I believe you mentioned wanting to fuck until we both pass out from exhaustion. Is that still your desire?"

She exhales and grins. "Without a doubt."

I grin and start cranking things up again. "Then ready yourself because I don't tire easily."

CHAPTER ELEVEN

Keyla

$\mathcal{I}$ wake with Doc's heavy arm wrapped protectively across my chest and I smile. I'm so thankful to have him in my life and my mating. When the soul-searing hit, everything happened so fast. There was me and Doc and then me and Creed and then Creed and Rhylan. It feels like we've been scrambling to sort out what that means from that first moment in the portal gate clearing.

I said it would be good for Creed to have a couple of days to sort through his emotions, but in all honesty, I need that too.

I don't regret anything about the four of us bonding, but maybe my age and inexperience have played a part in the learning curve. I saw what Kotah built with the quint and after a life with little or no love to nurture us, I wanted that too.

Was that greedy? Immature? Naïve? Maybe from an outside perspective, but I honestly think it was hope.

Mother was right—it sort of *is* Kotah's fault.

I might not have mated with both Creed and Dillan and then

Rhylan if I hadn't seen how Kotah's life flourished with the love and support of multiple mates.

Creed saw my love for Dillan and wanted me to be happy. I saw the same love in him for Rhylan and wanted him to be happy. Now, there are four of us and it's more complicated than I thought.

Then again, it's only been a couple of weeks.

I lay there, searching my heart and soul for any hard truths I need to face about it being a mistake.

There are none.

I love Doc. He is my first boyfriend and is attentive and loving and protective and we have fun together. When he makes love to me, I feel delicate and cherished and it's so easy to love him and his bear.

Everything with him is easy.

He accepts me unconditionally and loves me for who I am. He was the first person other than Kotah to give me that and holds a special place in my heart.

I love Creed, too. He and I share a similar background and understand one another the way only another royal could. Our soul-searing is a lock. We are both driven to lead the citizens of Dornte toward a future in which they feel safe. I'm excited for our relationship to grow both privately and professionally. Things with him are more complex than with Dillan but that's not bad.

Creed challenges me to be more than I am.

And then there's Rhylan. Creed loves him, so I'm looking forward to getting to know him better. Was I rash to invite him into our mating? Maybe. I still think it was the right thing to do. Rhylan has struggled with judgment and was forced to do the wrong things for the right reasons all his adult life. Even still he sacrificed it all for his love for Creed.

I love and respect him for that.

And though the man is guarded, the dragon seeks the life and love I've promised. My wolf has bonded to his dragon, and she has great instincts. I trust things will work out there.

With Rhylan, we need time, but love is budding.

"Hey, babe. Are you all right?" Doc's hazel eyes are half-open and he's reading my expression.

"Perfectly. Go back to sleep. I'm going to have a shower and check in across the hall. I want to spend some time with Kotah before we go back."

"Do you want me to get up?"

I press a hand against the morning scruff of his cheek and smile. "Nope. You're free to lounge. I have a few things to do around the palace before we head back."

"Sounds good. I could use another hour. You wore me out last night."

I brush a kiss across his lips and my heartbeat stumbles in my chest. "All my girly parts thank you. I loved last night. And yeah, you earned extra rest."

He winks and closes his eyes, his triumphant smile adorable.

I spend a few extra moments under the hot water, working out some sore muscles, and then dry off, get dressed, and head across the hall. Movement in the kitchen near the door tells me there's at least someone stirring, so I knock lightly and wait.

Calli opens the door. "Good morning, girlfriend."

"Hey, is Kotah up? I wanted to make a couple of stops in the palace this morning and thought he might like to join."

"He hasn't surfaced yet. Come in. I'm heating some of Maggie's cinnamon buns. Do you want one?"

"Hells yes. Maggie's cooking is one of the things I'll miss most of all living in the Fae Realm."

"Then we'll simply have to visit often and bring you care packages," Hawk says. The avian is dressed to impress and looking fine in his suit clothes.

Mmm... he smells like a healthy, horny male. "Oh, am I interrupting? I can go and come back."

Hawk leans in, kisses me on the cheek, and then waggles his brow at Calli. "No. Your arrival is perfect timing. If I didn't get out of here now, I would've missed a very important meeting."

Calli grins and hands him a mug. "I can't help it that you're insatiable."

Hawk rolls his eyes and accepts the coffee. "Like it was me instigating. You know every one of my buttons and enjoy pushing them."

Calli chuckles and smiles at me. "Guilty as charged. Okay, go be a corporate wonder. Love you."

"Love you more." He waves over his shoulder as he strides off toward the office.

I chuckle at the two of them and climb onto one of the barstools at the kitchen island. "So, things are going well?" I whisper.

Calli is smiling so widely she looks like she might burst. She puts two warm cinnamon buns onto a plate and tilts her head toward the door. "Shall we?"

"Sure. That works."

The two of us head out to the hall and she closes the door quietly behind us.

As we stroll down the private corridor toward the staircase, I reach over and pick up one of the gooey goodness cinnamon buns. Taking a bite, I groan and let the sugary delight wake my taste buds. "Oh my gods. No matter how many times I have one, there's no preparing for it."

"True story. And little Liza here loves them, don't you baby?"

I take another bite and grin. "Liza? I didn't know we had a name?"

"So far that's the only name they've agreed on. Liza was Hawk's mom and he wanted her to have a mention."

"That's nice." I finish chewing my breakfast and pause on the landing before we head down to the public section of the palace. "How are you and Hawk doing? I know a few weeks ago you were a little put out that he was making decisions for you in the bedroom. Have you made any headway there?"

Calli grins. "Just last night... and actually, you helped with that."

I sit down on one of the steps and she sits beside me. "Oh? How so?"

She sets the plate down and licks the sugar off her fingers. "Apparently, Doc mentioned to the boys how deciding what you could and couldn't handle in the bedroom blew up in his face. He almost lost you and then got a real kick to his male pride when Creed gave you what you wanted, and he realized his vision of you wasn't fair."

"Not to mention infuriating," I say.

"Exactly. Oh, I know. I was livid and hurt when Hawk put limitations on what he was willing to share with me."

"But you've worked through that now? He took you into the playroom?"

She nods. "Last night. We had so much fun, first just him and I, and then Jaxx came in too."

I clap my hands and let out a quiet squeal. "I'm so excited for you. Congrats. Another benchmark for you and your guys."

Calli nods. "Yeah. Hawk asked me to give him the time to let his guard down and it's paid off. He's more at ease now and he's truly settling into the emotional side of the mating."

"I'm so happy for you... for all of you."

"Thanks. Now, how's it going with your guys? Tell me everything."

Rhylan

After twenty minutes of explaining about the Blood Witch's treachery and how she made the same statement I've heard

Shadowcaster say more than once, my mother is still not convinced there's a connection.

"You know there's no affection between me and Shadowcaster, but I can't help you, Rhy. I stay as far away from that asshole as I can. I wasn't privy to his dealings with Laryssa and I don't know if he's connected with her witch."

"And would you tell me if you did?"

She arches a brow and I know I hit a truth with that.

"No. You wouldn't because I'm damaged goods and for you to put your neck out and help me puts you in the same predicament."

"Like I said. You're the smart one."

As much as I understand her stance, I can't say it doesn't hurt. No matter how old a kid gets there's still a part of him that wants to know there are people who will stand up for him at any cost. Parents are supposed to do that, aren't they?

My father did and it cost him his life.

Maybe she's smart not to risk herself for me.

"Well, I've said what I came to say," I say, glancing to the crevice that leads back to the main courtyard. "Are you sure you won't come with me? I'm mated to a king now. You can build a new life in Dornte where you're not the possession and plaything of an asshole like Shadowcaster."

She shakes her head. "You're thinking like a man and not a dragon. Maybe it's different for you because you've lived outside the lair for the past two years, but my dragon belongs here with its kin."

It's not different for me but I haven't been kin here for almost a decade. "If you change your mind, you know where to find me. The Thornebane Castle is hard to miss."

My mother cups my jaw and I bend for her to kiss my forehead. "Be well, Rhylan. May your dragon soar high and your heart remain free."

The pain in my chest brings tears to my eyes and I blink to

keep them from taking hold. I truly am exiled and she's saying goodbye to me. She's choosing an arrogant, brute of a manwhore over her son.

Lifting my chin, I let that settle over me. "Blessed be, Mother. May you find the peace and happiness you deserve."

I leave her without looking back and make my way through the twists of the rocky passage. When I get to the opening to the courtyard, I peek out to check that my way is clear and—

"Slecking hell."

Shadowcaster and a dozen of his ass-lickers are sitting in lawn chairs facing my exit drinking ale. "Oh, come now," Shadowcaster says. "Join us Rhylan. Settle a bet. We've been sitting here drinking and wondering how one dragon could be so impossibly stupid as to not only betray me and my orders but to then actively engage me in battle, ignore the serving of an exile disc, and then show his face in this lair. Is it swift passage to the after you seek? If so, you're in luck. You're about to get your wish."

I glance back down the rocky path leading to my family home but what's the use? There's only one exit and there's no way I'm reaching it.

Stepping out into the open of the courtyard, I hold my hands out to the side. "Hello, all. Imagine meeting you here."

Creed

Isabo and I work all morning in the King's Tower erasing any sign that Laryssa was ever here. We remove the furniture she moved in here and find my ancestral bedroom suite where it was stored in the cellar. When that's been brought up and set back into place, we box any of her things we think can be used by others, and then we burn the rest on the back lawn and let those who wish to celebrate dance around the pyre.

It's rather cathartic.

"Where's the elven rug the King Erringyle gave my father?" I say pointing to the bare hardwood in front of the fire. "Is it stashed somewhere?"

Xxani, the Castle Head of House nods. "Yes. During the confusion of the raid, your father instructed us to take all the irreplaceable items cataloged in his journal to the archive passage and secure them."

"Wonderful. Please see that they are returned to their proper places of honor."

The man fists a hand over his upper heart. "Yes, Majesty."

I stand back and smile at the progress. "Thank you all. It's looking much more like home by the hour. I leave you to it."

With the thought of sorting through the debris of the past two years firing my cells, I return to the heir's suite and head straight into my chamber. Pulling out the drawer where I stashed all of my Bloom momentos, I take it over to the bed.

Keyla was right. I need to come to terms not only with my feelings of guilt where Bloom is concerned but to put into perspective where my emotions lay now.

In my mind and my heart, I mourned and buried my sweet earth guardian years ago. Rhylan helped me through the physical aspects of that and then Keyla healed the emotional wounds.

Bloom was an important part of my life as Prince Creed, but King Creed is another man altogether. The universe saw the difference.

Now I do too.

I sort through the knickknacks I thought so important two years ago when she was taken from me. The ribbon she used to tie around her throat. The little notes she used to leave me on the mirror. A moon earring I found hooked into the loop of the rug when I collapsed on the floor in the early days of Laryssa's rule.

I look at the assembled pile of things and the only thing that runs through my mind is how much I want to finish this and be ready for when Keyla comes home.

Come home, Little Wolf.

It's important to me that she thinks of this castle as her home. I regret Bloom's suffering. I wish things had been different for her for a dozen reasons, but none of them are so that we could be together.

I love Keyla.

I love that she is secure enough in that to give me time to come to that end on my own.

I love that she recognized my feelings for Rhylan and both she and Dillan want to draw him in as an equal part of this relationship.

I love that she is not only the universe's solution to me reclaiming my throne, but she's also passionately invested in the citizens of Dornte.

I love her. Her youthful energy. Her fight and fire. Her wolf's strength and bravery.

Honestly, I'd be surprised if there was anything my little wolf was afraid of. She is a marvel, and the magic of our union grows stronger every day. She may have stepped back for me to sort through my anger about Bloom, but enough is enough.

I need her home where she belongs.

A knock on the outer door has me closing the distance to answer it when I catch the mental energy of Rhylan's twin in the corridor. Opening the door, I take in his expression, and I admit, I'm confused.

"Vikarus? What is it?"

He stares at me, his expression hard and pinched as he hands me a note. "He denies it, but I know you did something to mess with his head. This is on you, Creed. It's your fault."

When he turns and storms off, I'm left wondering what the hell he's talking about. Which, with Vik, isn't all that unusual.

Stepping back inside my suite, I unfold the parchment and read the words inked on the thick stock.

You are Invited.
What: The execution of Rhylan Silverwing
How: Flaying until death
Where: The Travon Lair
When: Sundown

My mind stalls out. Rhylan can't die. We're just getting started with our lives and he has so much to live for. I'll rally an army and... I have no idea where the Travon Lair is. No one does.

Fae species tend to be very protective about things and dragons more than most. To my knowledge, no one knows where the dragons live.

How do I even begin to find out?

Sundown. I check the time and curse. I have less than five hours to get to Travon, find the lair, and find a way to stop this execution.

CHAPTER TWELVE

Keyla

"So, I was thinking you'd be a perfect addition to my castle staff. They've been through so much, Shadow. Even if you only come with me temporarily, I know you can help so many of the Dornte citizens."

I sit back in the cushy chair in the castle's mental health wing and wait for an answer. Shadow, son of Nightshade, is a lovely urban elf with dark purple hair, deeply tanned skin, and the long, pointed ears of his race.

When it became obvious he would never be able to live among humans undetected, he chose to serve in the palace and make it his home. I don't know that he's been off the grounds in over a decade.

"And in the fae realm, you'll be free to explore and travel and take on any number of new adventures."

"And what are we to do?" Mother says, stepping into the meditation clinic. She frowns at me and her usual displeasure seems to be stronger than usual. "If you lure our people away from the castle, who do we turn to in times of need?"

I stand and face my mother, stepping between her and poor Shadow. "You have a counseling staff of six talented, empathetic, and dedicated professionals. I spoke to only Shadow and only because not only do I think he'd be a wonderful fit for Dornte, but I think Dornte would be a wonderful fit for him as well."

She flattens a hand over the silk bodice of her jacket and frowns. "We can discuss it further over dinner. I have an appointment with Sharina regarding my unresolved betrayal from Raven. I cannot deal with you and your needy whining right now."

"No Mother," I sigh. "Of course not. Please, don't let us hold you back. If Sharina's waiting, I'm sure you want to get yourself sorted."

"Tardiness is a sign of disrespect," she says, striding off toward the private offices. "Remember that Nakeyla."

"Yes, Mother."

When Shadow and I are alone once again, I take his hand and squeeze. "Think about it. I'm heading back tonight, but if that's too soon for you to join me, we can make arrangements to get you to Pennsylvania and through the gate. I truly think it's an opportunity to be considered. If you have family who wish to join you, I will make arrangements. Whatever you need."

Shadow dips his chin and stands when I stand. "Your intentions are well received, Princess. I thank you for your consideration. I shall consider it and get back to you promptly."

"Excellent. Thank you."

With a spring in my step, I head toward the palace kitchens. Adahy was right about my father being targeted and poisoned. We didn't listen and I owe her an apology.

She lost a great deal when she spoke out against Raven years ago. She lost her human form, her place as a weapon's master at the castle, and the respect of her peers. She's lived more than a decade, watching over Kotah and giving him the support he needed to be the man that he's become.

She is a silent hero.

I want to assure her the truth has now been exposed and we are so very sorry she suffered for standing against the evils of our world.

∼

Doc

While Keyla is busy doing her thing, I get ready for the day and head across the hall to spend an hour with Brant. The two of us never seem to get time to just hang out and shoot the shit anymore.

And since Keyla and I are headed back to the Fae Realm tonight, I figured my time is running out.

"So, things are turning around for you? You and Keyla are back on track?"

I lean over the pool table and line up my next shot. "Yeah. It took me a few days to wrap my head around polyamory, but I got there. Like Kotah says, multiple partners doesn't mean half the love it means double."

"What about Rhylan? Have you guys made it work with him, yet?"

I give my cue a quick snap and watch my targeted ball drop into the pocket. Grabbing the chalk off the side of the table, I make my way over to assess my options. "The four of us seem to be on the same page. Rhylan is still keeping his distance, but there's nothing overtly wrong. He's just going through a lot."

Kotah and Jaxx bring in a plate of hot, roast beef sandwiches on sourdough and my bear lets off a rumble of approval. I lean my cue against the table and join them at the covered poker table. "Thanks, guys. This smells awesome."

Jaxx sets a tray of sides down next to the sandwich tray and

Brant and I dig in. "I'll see if Hawk can join us for lunch. Be right back."

Brant hands out the plates and I take a couple of the sandwiches, some coleslaw, and reach for the horseradish. This is what I'm talking about.

Wildlings know how to feed wildlings. There is enough food here to feed the entire palace staff.

"Is there anything you need?" Kotah asks.

I set a cloth napkin over my lap and shake my head. "No. I'm good."

Kotah looks up from his plate and chuckles. "I meant anything that would make the transition to the Fae Realm easier for you and Keyla?"

"Oh, sorry." I take a big bite of my sandwich and think about that while I chew. "Actually, yeah. Keyla mentioned something to me, and I thought the idea had merit. I don't suppose she'll ask you, so I will."

Kotah brightens. "What is it?"

Jaxx and Hawk join us and the five of us settle in and chow down. "Keyla and I were talking about how the only downside to her mating and yours is that the two of you have destinies tying you to separate realms."

He frowns. "Agreed. I've been thinking a lot about that as well."

"Yeah, well, she's pretty sad about being separated from you. She was jazzed about being your right hand and running the realm with you. Now she has her own realm to run with Creed."

He nods. "Duty and destiny seem to have a way of restructuring our lives."

"What upsets her most is how if she wants to visit or we need you, we can get to the gate and here within fifteen or twenty minutes but then we have to arrange travel to the airport and then the flight back here. It's hours each way."

Kotah nods. "It's not ideal."

"Right. But then Keyla thought that since Hawk owns all that land in Pennsylvania anyway and you guys were wondering where to build your own Prime Palace, that maybe you'd consider building it in the forested area near the portal gate."

Kotah smiles. "I've been thinking the same thing. The forested area there is perfect for my wolf to run and I want to be actively involved with the integration and arrival of the Stone-Haven visitors."

Hawk pauses, his arm extended to claim a sandwich. "Yeah? Do you want a house built? A palace? An office? What have you got in mind, Wolf? I'll make it happen."

Kotah offers Hawk an adoring smile. "I was thinking something like the Northwood Lodge but built to suit our new needs. A private residence and then maybe a corporate center at a distance that's easy to get to but not so close that we can't escape the politics of the realm when we want to step away."

"Maybe with a connecting tunnel so we can come and go without notice," Hawk says, his eyes alight with the thought of spending an exorbitant amount of money to make his mates happy.

"Oh," Brant says. "If we have an underground tunnel, can we have a bunker area like on my ranch? Then we've got an emergency lockdown vault if we need it."

I laugh, shaking my head. "I think Keyla was just hoping that you'd have a home close enough so we can pop back and visit with you guys and spend time with the baby."

"It's not hot and tropical," Kotah says to Jaxx. "I know you were hoping for a location further south."

Jaxx waves that away. "So, we hop on the jet and fly to Aruba. S'all good. If it works for the family, it works for me."

Hawk nods. "Oh, yeah. I'm loving this idea. We'll have to clear it with Calli though. We've been talking about where to build our home base, so she'll want a say, but if she doesn't object, I'll have my architects flown in and we'll start surveying the land and drawing up plans."

"Oh, can I get a family cottage for Mama and Daddy?" Jaxx asks. "When the baby comes, they want to be close."

Hawk nods. "Of course. This afternoon we'll have a brainstorming session and we'll come up with our wish list. Sound good?"

I dip my wad of roast beef into the horseradish and laugh. "You guys are a riot. I've never seen people so excited to spend a million dollars."

Hawk grins. "You can't take it with you, Bear. Money doesn't buy happiness. It buys freedom and choices. If a couple of millions builds us the perfect home for our family to live and grow, I think that's money well-spent."

I lift my can of Coke and hold it up for a toast. "To money well-spent."

Brant, Jaxx, Kotah, and Hawk join me with their soda salutes. "To money well-spent."

Creed

It takes me half an hour to get to the Travon palace and my heart is thundering in my chest the entire way. The two men acting as my escorts—Elon and River—are frustrated with me and trying to keep up. "Majesty. Please allow us to lead the way. We are in an opposing quadrant."

The three of us are jogging toward the grand entrance of the palace, taking the wide, stone steps at a run two at a time.

"Travon hasn't been hostile toward us in over two hundred years," I say. "I'm not worried they'll think I'm attacking. If I were, I'd bring more than the two of you."

River seems to recognize the logic in that and focuses on his footing.

The sentinel at the door sees us coming and opens things wide before we get there. "King Creed," he says as I blow past him.

"Thank you," I call back over my shoulder. I don't take time to exchange pleasantries beyond that.

It's only once I'm through the public areas of the palace and closing in on the royal receiving room that I slow to catch my breath. Grabbing the pull-rope to call an attendant, I yank and swing the thing like I'm a kid sounding the dinner bell.

"King Creed," a halfling woman says, rushing into the room. She makes quick work of climbing the steps behind the reception desk so that she's meeting me at eye level. "How can I be of aid, sire?"

"Is Queen Yennith available for an emergency consult?" I emphasize the *emergency* part of that sentence, so she doesn't bother coming back at me with procedural bullshit about the protocols of calling a meeting. "If you could inquire promptly, I would appreciate it. It's a matter of great urgency."

"Yes, Majesty. I'll inquire at once." She doesn't bother with the steps down. Jumping off her platform, she lands on the floor and rushes through the doorway she used to enter.

When she returns a moment later, I get the sense I'm not going to like what she says. "Apologies, Majesty. The Queen is off the property at present. She's attending a ritual blessing in the highlands and is not expected back until tomorrow."

Fuck. "What about her son? Is Prince Satune here?"

"I believe so. One moment, I'll check."

Again, she shuffles off to the other room but this time when she returns, she doesn't look so grim. "He is. He is currently meeting with the Travon quadrant leaders and will be finished with the district governors within the hour."

Within the hour? I check my watch. Damn it, that's cutting

things close. Maybe I can send word to him and call him out early.

"Very well. Where is he? I'll make my way there now to save time."

"I'm happy to escort you, sire. Follow me."

~

Rhylan

My head lolls limply as I hang by the two hamburgered stumps I used to consider my wrists. I inventory the damage done and am proud of the thoroughness of my brethren. A dozen of my brood brother dragons took their cracks at me, leaving me a throbbing, swollen mass of broken flesh.

All hail the most powerful wildling race.

But the joke's on them because despite the stabbings and the pummelings and having half the males of the brood piss on me, I'm still sure I made the right call. I'm a male of honor and they're assholes.

Although, I keep that opinion to myself.

I cough on blood, hissing as the tensing of muscles releases another round of agony. This won't end well. My skin is on fire. I've lost too much blood. And no cavalry is coming because no one who gives a shit about me knows where this lair is.

The festering stench of burnt flesh, blood, and dragon piss singe my sinuses. The olfactory trifecta triggers my gag reflex and churns my stomach. It's a good thing I haven't eaten in a while, or I'd be retching and causing myself even more agony.

"Wonderful, you're awake." Shadowcaster steps into the cavern where I'm confined and grips one of the dagger hilts sticking out of my side. He twists it and then sends me spinning and swinging as the bindings on my wrist cut deeper.

My dragon fights its tether, but the electrical pulses they shot me with make it impossible for me to shift. When my spinning slows and my head settles enough to clear, I blink my swollen, watery eyes and try not to black out.

I can barely see past the swelling. All I've got is a tiny window of vision between the lids of my one eye as I swing round in a slow rotation looking at the same things over and over...

Asshole alpha looking smug as shit... blood spattered stone wall... One dragon guard... A second dragon guard... The rock crevice leading out of here... And back to my asshole alpha looking smug as shit.

"You remind me a lot of your father," Shadowcaster says. "He thought himself above our laws too."

He didn't. My father followed every arrogant and asinine order his alpha ever gave him. He simply lost control of his dragon when, despite his loyalty and commitment, that asshole moved in to claim his mate.

"Are you ready to atone for your sins? We're setting up for quite an event tonight. Invitations have been sent. The courtyard is being transformed. And a grand feast is being prepared."

"I committed no sin. I followed every order you and Laryssa gave me. She deemed me a traitor and tried to kill me without even speaking to me first. Was I supposed to sit there and die? I don't slecking think so."

His eyes flash a warning. "That's exactly what you'll do tonight. You'll accept your death with the honor of any noble dragon."

"Killing me isn't noble. It's petty revenge because my father challenged you and even with him gone for more than a decade, my mother still can't stand to have you touch her."

"You know nothing of my relations with your mother."

I roll my eyes and then regret it when pain shoots deep into my eye sockets. "You make her skin crawl. Hell, not just her. Half the women you force yourself on despise every moment of your awkward hump and thump."

The fist that rams into my intestines hits like a concrete block. "Bite your tongue, welp. I am your alpha."

"Not anymore, you're not. I've been exiled. For the first time in my life, I'm free to tell you how much everyone laughs at you behind your back. You're a joke. A pompous loser that bullies his people because if they didn't fear him they wouldn't follow—"

The wind is knocked out of me and my consciousness flags.

If nothing else... I'll go out speaking my truths.

CHAPTER THIRTEEN

Creed

"Thornebane, nice to see you out and about, my friend." Satune strides out of the parliamentary chambers, holding out his hand. When he gets close, he meets my gaze and stops in his tracks. "Slecking hell, what's with your eyes."

I sigh. "A souvenir from being cursed by the Blood Witch. We're working on breaking her hold and correcting them. Listen. I need your help and time is running out. Is there somewhere we can talk?"

Satune gestures toward a door to our right and the two of us step into a private parlor of some kind. "What is it, old friend. What's happened?"

He stands well over six feet tall, dressed in long, gold robes, adorned with the tanzanite gemstones mined in the Travon Fringelands. In the years since I've seen him, he's filled out across the chest and now wears his forest green hair to his shoulders.

His features are more elongated and leonine than a human's

and his eyes glow gold like a cat's and reflect the light when he glances around the room. I always found his animal nature unnerving as a kid.

I suppose me mating three wildlings is nature's way of making me rethink my prejudice. "You heard I was soul-seared to the Prime Princess of the Human Realm and her mate, yes?"

He nods. "Yes. It's the talk of the realm. Two mates. It's radical, for sure."

"Not as radical as me mating *three*, I suppose."

Satune straightens, his golden eyes glittering as he stares without blinking. "Oh, now you're just getting greedy. How big is your bed?"

I wave that away. "Our fourth is a member of the Travon Dragon Clans. His name is Rhylan Silverwing and he and his brother—"

"The dragon twins," Satune says. "Yes. I know of the Silverwing twins. I knew them when we were kids. They would accompany their father when he had business here at the palace."

"Right, well, long story short, Rhylan's alpha is an asshole and laid claim to his mother. Their father challenged him and was killed, and the twins fell to the mercy of Shadowcaster."

He frowns. "What does this have to do with me?"

"I'm getting to that," I say, holding up a finger. "Shadowcaster sold the twins into servitude to Laryssa and when I killed her last week and reclaimed my throne, Rhylan was declared a traitor."

"Uh-huh... this is sounding like a species domestic dispute."

I take out the invitation Vikarus gave me and hold it up for him to see. "Shadowcaster has taken my mate prisoner and intends to flay him to death in a few hours. It may be a domestic dispute, but it's about to be an all-out declaration of war. I want my mate back."

Satune curses and takes the invitation to examine it.

"Tonight at sundown at the dragon lair? I'm sorry, my friend. There's no way for me to help you even if I were to step in. No one knows where in the traverse the dragon lands lay and there isn't time to search for them. It will be sundown long before we find them."

I hear the truth in his words, but I can't accept it. "There has to be a way... there just has to."

The sympathy in Satune's gaze is enough to make me homicidal. I think he sees it in my eyes too because he takes a step back. "Okay. Let me escort my guests out and get changed. I'll be back here in ten minutes with our military advisor, and we'll see what we can come up with."

"Thank you. Yes. Apologies." I pace a few steps away and shake out my fists.

When I'm alone in the room, I try to get a hold of myself. We will save him. I love him. He won't be persecuted for doing what's right. Sitting on the edge of the upholstered bench by the wall, I run my hands down my thighs and try to rein in my mental energies.

I'm amped up.

Ever since I called forth the Amberloq power on the night of our searing and then Keyla connected with it last week during the battle against Laryssa, my cells have been alive with potential energy.

Something about that tweaks my curiosity. Is there any way Honor's Amberloq warriors or their power could help track down a hidden lair of asshole dragons?

Keyla

My morning with Calli is time well spent and by lunch, we've spoken to everyone I needed to speak to. The two of us return to the royal residence and I pack two large trunks of personal belongings from my rooms to take with me to my new life.

"Are you sure you don't want this cutie?" Calli asks, waving at me with the stuffed arm of Ms. Penelope, my stuffed wolf.

"I don't suppose the queen of a quadrant needs to be snuggling her stuffies at night."

Calli snorts. "Not with the three mates you've got."

I grin. "Why don't you keep Ms. Penelope for the baby's room. Maybe she'll think of me now and then when I'm too long in a far away realm."

Calli sticks out a lip and makes sad eyes at me. "That's a sad story, girlfriend. Too bad it ain't happening. There's no way this baby won't know who you are. We'll see you guys all the time, I promise."

A knock on my bedroom door brings one of the original staff to my father's reign. "You called for me, milady?"

"Yes, Gemmy, thank you for coming. Will you see that these get to Mr. Barron's jet right away? We are leaving tonight, and I want to ensure my things don't hold up our departure."

"Yes, Princess, ah… sorry, shall I address you as Queen Thornebane now?"

The worry on the royal porter's face is priceless. "You've known me my entire life Princess Nakeyla, so you choose. Both are correct. In this realm, I am and will always be your princess. In the Fae Realm, I am Queen Thornebane. There is no wrong answer."

He dips his chin in a quick nod. "Thank you, Princess. It's such a shame to see you go. You have always been the sweetheart of the realm. I hope the people of Dornte realize how lucky they are."

I squeeze the man's wrist. "You flatter me."

Gemmy grips the handle of the trolley I've loaded and away he goes. Once he's off, I take another few minutes to look through my drawers. "Do you mind if I pack a bag to leave with you guys? You can stuff it in a closet or something, but honestly, the way the universe conspires for us to run off at a moment's notice, it would be nice if I—"

A buzz lights off in my head and I cup my temples and let off a hiss.

"Keyla, what's wrong?" Calli's hands close around my shoulders and squeeze. "Talk to me, hon. What's happening?"

I breathe through the intensity of my mating beacon exploding and then wince at her, holding my forehead. The current is there again, zapping through me like I've touched an exposed wire. "Something's wrong. I need to get back to the Fae Realm. My mating beacon is going haywire."

~

Doc

"How's she doing?" Brant asks as I sink into one of the four leather captain's chairs in Hawk's jet.

Jaxx hands me a drink and I suck it back—one and done. I hand him the empty and he tops me up.

I'm about to go the same route with round two and think better of it. If Keyla's beacon is going wild because Creed and Rhylan are under attack and need our help, it won't do anyone any good for me to be half-plastered. "Kotah's working his magic and lying with her. He's trying to calm her mind but she's in rough shape."

"And we're too fucking far from the portal gate to be effective," Hawk snaps. "It won't happen again, I promise you that."

Jaxx leans over the back of Hawk's chair and kisses the top of his head. "This is not your fault, hotness."

Lukas strides down the aisle from the cockpit and sighs. "We need to create a portal link from the new gate room to the palace. This commute is getting old fast."

"Too late," Hawk says, frowning. "I'm making the new Pennsylvanian Prime Palace a priority."

"Say that five times fast," Brant says, chuckling. "How long until we land?"

Lukas checks his FCO watch and shows us the readout. "Fourteen minutes. I've got the helicopter prepped and ready and Gantley is working on the new configurations."

"Do you think it'll work?" Calli asks.

Hawk shrugs. "I don't see why not. It works in the Fae Realm. As Creed said, it's the same concept as transporting people, just without the bells and whistles."

Jaxx chuckles. "And since we haven't gotten to the bells and whistles part of our portal travel, what's the difference?"

I take another long sip of my drink and let the amber fire burn its way down my throat. "Yeah, I just wish our trial run wasn't at a moment when Keyla's alarm bells are going off and we don't have any clue what we're walking into."

Brant holds up a meaty fist. "Preach."

Rhylan

I have no idea how long I've been playing the part of the dragon chandelier. By the time the chains are released and I'm lowered to the ground, I can't feel my arms, my body is trembling with blood loss, and I've given up the fleeting hope that either my mother or my brother give enough of a shit about me to help.

So, this is it.

The unfortunate part of dying here with my face mutilated is that I can't even look the assholes in the eye as they put me to death.

The swelling over my eyes has gotten progressively worse over the past hours and now, if I care to witness my demise, I can only see out of a tiny sliver out of my right if I force it open. Yay me.

"Hose him down," Shadowcaster says somewhere behind me. "He reeks."

"That's what happens when people use you for pissing target practice." I chuckle at my quip, proud that my voice is steady. I can't move to get up, but my hands have ceased ripping off my wrists, so I take that as a win. "Time to whip your big dick out and get your revenge, big man?"

A boot drives into my stomach and I curl around it like a shrimp in a boiling pot.

"Your execution is about justice, not revenge. You betrayed your oath. You violated our traditions by coming back here after your exile. You're not fit to live as a dragon from this brood."

A long, dark chuckle rumbles from my chest. "And here I thought it was because you hate me. My mistake."

"Oh, there is no mistake. I *do* hate you. I've known from the night I killed your father that we'd end up here. You've never given me the respect I deserve."

"Respect is earned, not deserved."

A biting stream of cold water hits my shoulder and knocks me tumbling over the grit of stone. How he thinks hosing me while I'm rolling in the dirt will get me cleaner for his big event is just another example of his dim wit.

When the water stops, I roll onto my ass, sputtering and laughing. "So, how do I look now. All clean?"

"Get him off the ground," Shadowcaster snaps. "I'm bored of this. Get him to the stocks and lock him in."

I'm yanked to my feet. When the meathead on my right hits one of the daggers still sticking into my side my legs give away and I almost black out.

"On your feet, traitor," a graveled voice says.

"Oh, hey, Narkor. How are things? Hey, since I'm going to die and all, tell your sister she is by far the greatest lay of all the dragon females in this brood. She'll appreciate knowing that."

I'm ready for the gut-punch but it was worth it.

Narkor is such a sanctimonious prick.

"You can't bait me, traitor. There's no way out of this for you."

"Who wants out of it? Bring it on, asshole. Let's get 'er done."

Someone unlocks my shackles and grips me by the elbows. "As you wish, Silverwing. Your audience awaits."

My feet hang heavy with each step I take, the pace a pitifully slow death march. The pads of my feet become more scored and torn on the jagged rock with every step, and I'm not entirely sure I won't black out again.

Damn, I've been on the receiving end of dragon beatdowns before but those were just bully hazings for shits and giggles.

Today my brethren have their A-game focus on.

"A little sore, are you, Silverwing?" Narkor asks.

Every piece of landscape I own hurts but there's no way I'm going out showing weakness. I'll make it to the stocks by stubborn will and a sense of pride, because who are we kidding... that's all I've got left.

I've never given much thought to the fae ability to heal. Vikarus and I have done the dance of bruised and broken so long—first as hated members of the brood and then as soldiers —that I stopped feeling the pain. But this torture stuff is next-level agony.

It's humbling—not to mention, it sucks.

I sense when we exit the crevice and venture out into the open space of the courtyard. The temperature of the air drops and being naked and dripping wet is suddenly even less fun. I fight the urge to buck against the arms securing me, but honestly, where would I go?

I can't see. I can't fly. And by the strength of the whispered murmurs all around me, the entire brood has gathered.

Right. Shadowcaster said he sent out invitations.

With my limited sliver of sight, I scan the attendees to find Vikarus or my mother. If they're here, I want to look them in their eyes.

I don't see them.

My dragon surges inside me with enough force to affect my footing. I stumble and the grips on me tighten. I feel the heat of gazes on me, everyone coming out to enjoy the show.

Slecking assholes.

Fine. If they want a show, I'll give them one. "Yes, I mated King Creed of Dornte. Yes, you're about to assassinate a member of Dornte royalty. And yes, I'm quite sure he and my other mates and the Phoenix Quint will come here and retaliate."

"We're not afraid of them," someone shouts off to my right.

"Then you're either arrogant or an idiot. Vikarus and I got our asses handed to us by Calli alone. Then, she held off a horde of you at Laryssa's compound. She had no trouble putting a dozen of you in your place. Imagine what will happen when she's pissed."

"There are twenty-seven of us," Shadowcaster says. "I'll take those odds."

I chuckle. "You'll be bugs swatted out of the sky, but yeah, keep telling yourself that dragons are the top of the hierarchy. That will make it easier for Calli to avenge my murder."

Our entourage arrives in the center of the courtyard, and I force my working eye open. So, it all comes down to this. Drawing a deep breath, I accept my fate.

"Lock him down," Shadowcaster says. "Let us end this and get to the celebration."

I watch my footing as I climb the wooden steps of the platform and lean forward to rest my neck and arms into the dips of the stocks. When I'm settled in place, the top plank is brought down and secured. The metal lock scrapes the loop of the coupling ring as it's laced through and then it snaps shut.

I am well and truly secured.

Straightening as much as possible, and with all eyes upon me, I clear my throat. "I, Rhylan Silverwing, former heir to the Silverwing legacy admit to falling in love and protecting my honor despite orders to the contrary. I sided with the fae universe over a hateful queen and I'm glad Dornte is free of the Blood Witch."

Shadowcaster laughs beside me. "Please. You can't honestly be so stupid to believe you have an ounce of honor. You are the exiled son of a traitor."

"And the Blood Witch isn't finished with Dornte," a female voice says just out of my line of sight. "Creed and his supporters may think they've won, but they have yet to feel the wrath of a scorned witch."

I fight to see who is speaking. It can't be the witch. Never has there ever been a non-dragon within the protected sanctum of the dragon lair.

"Who's there? There's no need to hide. I'm about to die a horrible death anyway, so show yourself."

Snap.

I close my eyes and stiffen as the flesh on my back ignites into a fierce burning. Barbed leather straps wrap around my ribs and cut into my skin. My vision fails me as the world goes black and I fight to stay conscious.

Shadowcaster has always liked a good flaying.

I lock my knees to hold my weight and swallow to clear my throat. "Have your fun, asshole. When I die, you better believe I'll come back to haunt all of you."

Snap.

Shadowcaster laughs behind me as another round of barbs tears at my flesh. "You never did know when to shut your mouth, Rhylan."

Snap.

I press my lips together and pant through my nose to keep

from crying out. I won't give him the satisfaction. When the sharpness of the pain ebbs, I call out. "Tell me, female. How do you see the witch taking her revenge out on Creed when he's the most powerful leader Dornte has seen in years?"

Snap.

"Come on, bitch. What can it hurt to tell me? I'm dead anyway, right?"

I swivel my view to catch sight of the woman who spoke before, but between the swelling of my eyes, the blood matting my hair down to my face, and my vision fritzing in and out from being flogged with a cat o' nine tails whip, I've got nothing.

Snap.

My dragon growls as a river of heat runs down my hips and thighs. I'm not going to survive this. Slecking hell. "Are my mother and twin here watching this? I hope you're enjoying the show. As my mates would say, fuck you."

Snap.

Broken-hearted, I let my head fall forward and prepare myself for my untimely end. There are so many things I regret or wish I'd taken the time to enjoy.

I've always wanted to learn to play the guitar well. And Keyla... I should've accepted her affection. I have a feeling that feeding from her while the two of us were joined and making love would've been magnificent. Oh well. Maybe in my next life.

I think I was afraid to let her become more than Creed's mate to me. If I accepted her, I had to live up to what a female like her deserves. With everything going wrong with my life, I didn't think I could do that.

Snap.

I grunt as the pain sears me to the bone. Case in point. Things haven't worked out well for me in the past decade.

A booming crash sounds in the distance and absently, I wonder what could make such a thundering noise. Then there's a steady *thunky-clunk-thunk* of stone raining to the ground and I try to remember the last time we had a rockslide within the lair.

Lost as I am from pain and waxing philosophical, it takes a moment for the scrambling and screeching around me to register.

My hair whips around in my face as a rhythmic *chuff-chuff-chuff* drowns out the screaming.

Then, a heavy *whoosh whoosh* of leathered wings joins the chaos.

Wings are nothing to cause panic in the lair of dragons, so what has them all...

Streams of hot, flame wash over the crowd.

In the back of my mind, it seems odd that the fire is gold and orange instead of the icy blue of dragon fire.

Two men on the platform burst into flame right in front of me. I chuckle as Narkor burns and I start to put it together. "I told you they'd be pissed off. Ladies and gentlemen, may I introduce to you my mates, the Phoenix of the Human Realm, and her Guardians."

Laughter bubbles up my throat and I honestly don't care if I die. Watching my brood burning and losing their shit is worth the price of admission.

Life is good.

CHAPTER FOURTEEN

Keyla

*H*awk's twin-engine Eurocopter AS365 Dauphin hovers in the air above the massive hole Lukas and Doc just blew in the side of a mountain. It took four military-grade RPG rockets to crack us a hole big enough to get inside but once the stone gives way and we see inside, I know my beacon led me to the right place.

"Nicely done boys," I say, shifting out of my seat and clicking onto the rappel line. "Now, let's get our dragon."

We had enough tactical training with Lukas during Calli's quest of opening the portal rift that we're all confident in a quick descent for battle. I lower myself out of the helicopter and wrap my fingers around the grip. "Little Wolf away."

Dropping for the open courtyard below, I go over my training in my head. I start the braking process when I'm halfway to the ground. Releasing the tension on the rope, I move my brake hand out at a 45-degree angle to regulate the rate of descent.

When my boots hit the ground, I clear the rappel rope through the ring until the rope is free and I step off.

I call my shift and my wolf is more than ready to respond. She digs in and we bolt through the scramble of people who set up lawn chairs to watch the public torture of my mate.

Calli's phoenix lets off a shriek and I hear the disgust in her voice. She blows out a steady stream of fire, igniting two men on the stage next to the bleeding male I can only assume is Rhylan.

Sweet Powers, look what they've done to him.

Violent roars from angry bears rumble on my left. I smile over at Doc and Brant doing their thing. Jaxx and Kotah are on my right, pushing back the women and children so they don't get involved in this battle. Hawk and Lukas are propped at the door of the helicopter their MP5s raised and firing in short bursts to provide cover fire from incoming forces.

Not that there are a lot of incoming forces. Calli has the men well pinned. Still, they're dragons, so we're ready for them on the ground and in the air.

When I arrive at the platform, I recognize Rhylan's scent before I recognize the man. He's naked and bleeding badly, the flesh on his back, shoulders, ass, and thighs covered in blood.

I shift back so I can use my hands to break him free.

"Rhylan, you're safe now. We're here. Today is not your day to die." I'm scrambling to find something to break the lock. The only thing around us are rocks. I grab a large one and start beating on the metal. "And me here without a lockpick."

Rhylan's mumbling something but his words are indistinguishable.

I try a few more times to smash the lock but get nowhere. Growling, I check my surroundings and see nothing that can help.

"It's okay, Rhy. I'm not giving up. I'll get you out of here and—"

"Here." A blonde woman rushes forward and holds out a metal pry bar. "Use this."

I take the tool from the woman and make short work of the brackets holding Rhylan hostage. When the brackets are open and I fling back the top section of the stocks, I ease Rhylan back to help him sit.

He's agitated, shaking his head and mumbling something I can't quite catch.

Brushing his hair out of his face, I fight back the tears pushing at me. "Shhh... you're safe now. I've got you. Just breathe."

$\sim$

Creed

It's past dusk when I race through a maze of rocky caverns in the Travon Traverse, and I pray to the gods I'm not too late.

Satune is with me, and he's brought a Travon military troop with orders to help me recover my kidnapped mate. If I'm right, and my beacon led us to where we need to be, these are the secret tunnels of the dragon clans.

It can't be much farther.

My heart is racing triple time as my muscles burn with the exertion of climbing the three-hundred feet up to the entrance. If I had my fucking wings, I could've flown, but without them, I was left with little choice.

Even thinking of them makes my back ache.

But honestly, when *doesn't* my back ache?

My boots crunch against the rubble and debris, but I don't slow. Rhylan's sentencing of death was at sundown. I can't fail him.

Racing around a bend, I stop short and glare at Vikarus blocking my path. "Get out of my way, Vik. I don't want to take you down but if I have to choose between you and your brother, there's no question."

Vikarus rolls his eyes. "Don't be stupid. Why do you think I gave you the invitation? Why do you think I volunteered to take sentry duty? I've done everything I can to pave your way here to help him."

"Other than telling me where we needed to come. Do you know how much time I wasted trying to find this place?"

"It would forfeit my life if I told you. You're here now. Are you willing to waste more time by arguing the point?"

Good point. Pushing past him, I stare at a tunnel with three branches. "Where am I going?"

"Two lefts and then straight until you come to the courtyard. You'll find him there. It's already started."

I don't look back. If it's already started, I don't have the time to waste on Rhy's asshole brother.

I race along the passageway and take the first left. As much as I detest the thought of people gathering around to enjoy the flaying of my mate, it works in our favor. Other than the one sentry at the entrance of the lair and Vik, we haven't seen or heard one other dragon.

A booming crash erupts up ahead and I look back at Satune. "Tell me these mountains aren't on a fault line or a volcano or anything."

Satune shakes his head. "Nothing that I know of."

A second boom hits and I shift to the wall of the cavern and chunks of stone break loose from far above. They rain down around us, forcing us to press tight against the sharp, stone walls.

"What do you think that was?" he asks.

"I don't know but if the mountain is about to collapse on top of us, I'd like to get my mate and be gone before it does."

"Agreed. I'm far too precious to be crushed by rocks like some unlucky miner."

"You are far too something." I get back to navigating the tunnels and have to remind myself. Do I have another left or am I supposed to go straight through on this one? "Fucking hell."

"Left," calls a voice from the shadows behind us.

I can't think about Vik right now.

He's caused more damage than he's worth by meddling in mine and Rhylan's life.

Up ahead, screams break out and I scramble to make sense of what's happening. Then I hear the rhythmic *chuff-chuff-chuff* of rotor blades.

I've only heard that sound once before.

"What the slecking hell is that noise?" Satune shouts over the growing din.

"It's called a helicopter. Keyla's family uses it to travel through the air in the Human Realm."

"How'd it get here?"

I grin, my heart bursting with pride. "I would bet my life that my queen has something to do with it."

"Queen's polish their nails and host political balls. They don't lead insurgencies into dragon lairs."

I chuckle and race forward, more eager than ever to get to the courtyard ahead. "*My* queen does."

Doc

Brant and I battle shoulder-to-shoulder and I can't help but enjoy myself. Dragons are strong and tough to back down but they're also over-confident and caught off guard with us attacking them within their lair.

Calli lets off a shriek above and I turn to check on her. Three dragons have taken flight and are challenging her position between them and us.

As they get close, the hiss of another rocket being launched lets loose.

The missile erupts from the helicopter and explodes on impact, knocking a black dragon hurtling toward the jagged shards on the ground.

I bark a grumbled laugh and go back to fighting. Hawk has an entire crate of rockets in the helicopter. He can defend his woman all night and have fun doing it.

We are almost finished with our opponents when Creed's spicy scent tickles my nose. I lift my head and follow the air currents back to an opening in the stone.

Hello mate.

After checking that Brant has things under control, I book it across the courtyard to escort him. Running on all fours is liberating and nothing gets the blood pumping like a true battle with a worthy enemy.

Dragons are stupid enough to think themselves untouchable. *Wrong.*

I close the distance to Creed and his group, giving it hard. I put on the breaks at the last moment and grin at the looks of terror filling the eyes of his men.

Creed sinks his fingers into the ruff of my neck and chuckles. "You're lucky I told them not to fire at anything other than dragons, Bear. You're quite a sight bearing down in a full run."

I smile up at the military men and then nudge him. When our communication link opens, I wink at him. *Are you flirting with me? Because if you are, I'm free after we get the hell outta here.*

Looking forward to it. Now, let's get what we came for and get home.

The two of us strike off toward Rhylan and Keyla and I'm struck, yet again by the bonds that have formed.

This is right.

This will work.

I genuinely care about Rhy and Creed and I'm head over

heels in love with Keyla. All we need is for the world to slow down for a bit so we can catch our breath.

Creed launches up the steps onto the platform and drops to his knees. "Imagine finding you two here." He pauses with his hands out, seemingly unsure of where to touch our dragon mate. "Fuck, Rhy, you're a mess."

"Wasn't me. I like rough but he was like this when I found him," Keyla jokes, her voice clogged with tears.

I shift back and take my time, assessing the dragon's injuries and then clock his pulse and track his pupils. "He's a little out of it and his adrenaline is keeping him from going into shock, but his injuries are primarily surface damage and likely psychological."

"You mean from being sold out and beaten by his own family and friends?" Creed snaps. "Imagine that."

Alrighty then, Creed's having some psychological difficulties of his own. "He's good for us to move. Let's get him back to that hole in the mountain. Hawk and Lukas will send down a rescue litter to get him up into the helicopter."

Keyla scoots back to give us room. "The most recent damage is on the back of his body. Maybe a shoulder carry would be the least painful?"

"Yeah, I can do that. It's going to hurt like hell, Rhy, and I'm sorry about that."

Rhylan is upset and mumbling something incoherent. I pull back and look at Creed and Keyla. "Are either of you getting that? What's he trying to say?"

Keyla frowns and then I feel her presence on our mental channel. *Rhy? Can you tell us what's wrong, sweetie? Are you hurting?*

Blood Witch. She's here. She was here.

Creed stiffens and searches the courtyard. *Where, Rhy? Where did she go?*

Don't know... Couldn't see.

Okay, Keyla says, scanning the chaos. *It's fine. The boys will look once we get you secured. Let's focus on you first.*

I straighten, press my fingers under my tongue, and let off a whistle. "Jaxx, we need you."

The jaguar races forward, his tail swinging behind him as he runs. He shifts on the fly as he reaches us, and I lean in close when he bends to assess Rhy. "Tell your mates the Blood Witch was here during Rhylan's torture. I don't know if she's still here, but if she is, let's not waste our chance."

Jaxx nods and his gaze softens as it does when they speak telepathically. A moment later, he blinks and focuses on us. "Hawk is sending Lukas down and I will tend to Rhy in the helicopter. The rest of you are on witch duty."

I help lift Rhylan onto Jaxx's shoulder and brush the bloody mat of his hair away from his face. "You'll be fine, mate," I say, pausing an extra moment to reassure myself that I'm right. "Jaxx is a paramedic and we've got phoenix tears waiting for you on that bird. Don't worry about a thing. We've got you."

Keyla cups his face and gives him a quick kiss on the cheek and then Creed does the same.

As Jaxx strides off toward the helicopter, I fight to draw a deep breath. "I just want a few days of us settling in and fooling around. No curses. No murder. No one trying to kill us."

Creed meets my gaze and the purple circles beneath his eyes stand out in stark relief from his pale, ivory skin. "Me too, Bear. Me too. Let's end this and get home."

That thought seems to settle some of Creed's more violent impulses and the next few minutes signal the change from a direct offensive and rescue to us regrouping and getting strategic.

The fight is winding down.

I think it was a blow to the dragons' egos that not only have we invaded their super-secret home base, but we did it easily. Many of the males started off in offense but when Calli torched a couple, they switched to defense and ushered their females and young to safety.

Not that the females and young would ever be in danger from us, but hey, it worked to our advantage.

Calli lets off an all-clear, flaps her wings, and flies into the helicopter. Shifting as she goes, she boards the chopper on a run in her human form.

"Hot damn, that was impressive," I say to Brant.

He grins. "She's come a long way since plowing ruts in fields with her face."

"True story," Keyla says.

A tall, fancy-pants guy with dark green hair and golden eyes steps up to the group.

Everyone tenses and Creed holds out his hands. "It's fine. Satune is the Prince of Travon and helped me get here. He's on our side."

Satune presses a fisted hand to his heart as a sign of respect and bows. "It is a pleasure to see you again King Northwood. My men and I are at your service."

Lukas doesn't seem to care. The mage doesn't like fresh blood on our teams and has made no secret about it in the past. "Thanks, that's great. Now, let's track down the Blood Witch and end this. We capture her, we break her curses. Creed and Keyla, are your beacons telling you anything?"

They take a moment to reach into themselves.

Keyla frowns and shakes her head. "My mind's gone quiet."

"Mine as well," Creed says.

Lukas pulls a plastic baggie out of the thigh pocket of his military pants. "Keyla and Kotah are likely more reliable anyway. I borrowed this from the witch's condo. Track her scent Northwoods. We'll do the rest."

Keyla and Kotah grin and a moment later, they have taken wolf form. They lift their noses and take a long whiff of the lady's scarf in the bag.

Give us a sec, Keyla says on our private channel. *The witch has been here a few days and there are overlapping trails.*

Creed relays that to the others and we wait while the two of them zigzag, nose down.

"There are two distinct trails," Keyla says, shifting back and standing tall. "Both used within the last hour."

Lukas frowns. "I'd rather not split up but I don't see any other option. I'll go with Kotah and Brant and follow this passage. Creed, Keyla, and Doc, you take that one. If it comes to a standoff, holler and I'll come running."

CHAPTER FIFTEEN

Creed

*M*y need for vengeance can't take much more. I never considered myself a violent man before Laryssa invaded my home and my life. I thought killing her, or standing there while Lukas killed her because I couldn't, would put out this burning darkness in me.

It hasn't.

If anything, finding Bloom and Honor the way we did has made me angrier.

I actively want to hurt, maim, and kill the people who have wronged me and the people I love.

First there's Rhylan and Vikarus's alpha, Shadowcaster, who forced them to betray not only their instincts but also each other in an effort to bankrupt them of any family pride they might still hold. Then, when Rhylan stands his ground, he exiles him and sentences him to death by flaying.

Then, there's the Blood Witch, who apparently is Shadowcaster's ally?

How twisted is that? Did she portal here when Lukas shot

her and she threw herself out the window? Is she fully recovered because he offered her refuge from the world she torments? That female sucked Bloom dry of her essence, trapped Honor in some kind of coma, and cursed me with a soul-consuming beast.

She must die.

"Creed? We're here, my prince," Keyla says, her hand resting on my shoulder. "We all understand what's at stake. You aren't alone in your fury but emotion in battle breeds mistakes. Focus on what needs to happen and it will happen. We will win the day. You'll see."

Honestly, if it was anyone else offering me that kind of reassurance, I might punch them in the face, but it's not. It's Keyla.

And for some reason, when she says it, I believe her... or at least, I want to believe her.

"I love you, Little Wolf. I'm so sorry about before... with Bloom."

She shakes her head. "Not here. Not now, my love. I understand completely. I always did. Now, focus and we'll kiss and make up when we leave this place."

How did I ever deserve her? "I understand what you're saying but I need to hold you, if only to stabilize my world for a moment."

Doc flashes me an impatient look, but I can't help that. I need to connect with her. Pulling Keyla into my arms I squeeze her tight to my body and breathe her into my lungs. Her calming effect works on me almost instantly.

Easing back, I kiss her forehead and send up a prayer of thanks. "All right. Thank you."

Her wolf's playful growl soothes my soul. "A couple who slays together stays together."

I chuckle and fall in behind her. "Track us a witch, my love. Let's end this."

Keyla

In my wolf form, I track the scent of the Blood Witch, and now that I understand her scent more, there's no way I'll ever forget it. At first, it puzzled me because I thought it was maybe a combining spell or something to throw me off. There are no less than eight significant separate species woven into the one scent and now I understand why.

Bloom wasn't the first fae she desiccated for power.

I have no idea how old this witch is but it doesn't matter. Her siphoning of life essence, whether it be for power or longevity, is over.

Her bonus time is over.

Her violence is over.

We jog along the ribbon of passageways, and I think about what it would've been like for Rhylan to grow up here. As a child, he probably loved playing in these seemingly endless passageways with the other children.

Before his alpha claimed his mother, at least.

He said after that, he and Vik were regarded as the unwanteds of the brood—the begotten of the traitor.

Never again. Once we take him home and heal him. He'll never again feel like a second-class citizen.

We come to a crossroads of two passageways and meet up with a woman and her daughter. The woman pulls the girl behind her, and I shake my head.

"We're not here for you," Creed says, gesturing for her to stand back as he, Doc, and three of Prince Satune's men follow me deeper into the mountain.

As we go, the scent gets fainter and fainter and I stop and shift back. "No. The scent is dying out not getting stronger. The witch bitch is not this way."

Creed curses and we turn around to leave.

The moment we do, I catch a surge of triumph in the air and

raise my hand. "Hold."

There is someone here. I smelled the smug confidence when I suggested we leave. I think it's a glamor.

I'll call Lukas, Dillan says, raising his FCO watch to send a message.

Creed, can you reach through it and find the mental signature?

Creed

I consider Keyla's question and close myself off from the anticipation and distractions of hunting down the Blood Witch. I calm my mind as much as I can, but it's only when Keyla slides her hand against mine and closes her fingers around my hand that I make any progress.

I've got you, my prince.

I draw a deep breath and let Keyla's calming nature wash over me. Touching her is the balm my soul needs. With her at my side, I can achieve anything.

Closing my eyes, I block out the world: my anxiety about Rhylan and the people who hurt him, the sounds of this strange place, and the knowledge that strangers are watching me, waiting to see if I can do this.

You can, Keyla says.

When she speaks the words, I believe her.

Searching the air around us, it's not so much what I find that's interesting, but what I don't find. In a rocky, natural space, there's an area of nothingness that I wouldn't have noticed if Keyla wasn't so in tune with her surroundings.

Facing the odd void, I strip away what I can, and then Lukas is there with the other half of our team.

The human mage steps in beside me and raises his palms.

"Well done. You almost got it. Weapon's up, people. Ready for anything."

Brant and Doc move in with the strange weapons I saw them use in the Human Realm. Keyla called them Glocks but I'm not sure if that's what they are or a brand of what they are.

It takes Lukas little time to remove the final layers of the glamor and then it's wavering before us. At last we're facing the Blood Witch and an arrogant male I assume is the dragon alpha.

"We meet again bitch," I say.

When she lifts her hands to strike out, Lukas steps in and counters her attack. Before she gets anywhere or has the chance to portal out of here like she's done twice already, I brace myself and focus on ending her.

The safeguards forced upon me to keep me from killing her trip and I feel my intentions powering down like before.

But this isn't like before.

Lukas worked with me all week peeling away the layers of her cursed spell. Keyla squeezes my hand and I'm filled with a rush of magic. We still aren't sure what her powers are or where they're coming from, but she's a force to be sure.

With the infusion of her power, my cells ignite. My blood boils. All I can see is the witch's death.

It builds in me like hot magma forcing its way up the core of a volcano. It feels like I'm breaking apart, my mind and body unable to contain the overload of power.

Die. For what you did to me. For what you did to Bloom. And for what you've done and plan to do to others. You. Must. Die.

"She's gonna blow," Lukas shouts, signaling for everyone to step back.

And she does.

With a hideous scream, she drops her attack and grasps her head. Her skull is unable to withstand the pressure of my attack and her cranium explodes. Blood and chunks of brain and bone detonate like a bomb.

Then, her body falls to the ground in a bloody heap.

It is done.

Shadowcaster's shock morphs into worry and then fury. "How dare you kill a guest in my lair. You'll hang for this, Creed. You might be a king in your quadrant but you're nothing here."

The dragon growls and steps forward to strike.

Satune's men tense and raise their blasters.

"Stop," Satune says from the back of the group. "You won't take your grievances out on Creed."

"Says who?" Shadowcaster growls.

"Says the Prince of Travon." Satune steps out from behind the shield of men and grins. "You've been hiding behind powerful women too long, Dragon. It's not very kingly of you."

"Or smart," Lukas says, grinning. "When your friends dominate with violence and brute force, you have to expect there will come those who oppose them."

"He thought himself safe, tucked away in his mountain," Keyla says. "The secret sanctum of the wildling dragons has kept you and your ancestors free from retribution for too long."

His gaze narrows on Keyla and everything in me wants him to pay for whatever unkindness he's thinking. "My alliance with the witch and Queen Laryssa broke no laws. I saw an opportunity and took it."

"That's not true," Vikarus says, sidling in from the shadows. "The secrecy of our home is the number one tenet in our lives. Allowing an outsider into our sanctum is punishable by immediate death. A non-negotiable offense written into our laws. By offering the Blood Witch safe harbor here, he condemned himself to die."

"Good to know," I say. "Then the only question is, who gets to exact the sentence?"

Shadowcaster's gaze narrows. "You can't kill me. You're not from Travon. You've invaded my sanctum and therefore are terrorists. Satune, you know I'm right."

"Do I?" Satune says, lifting his shoulders. "You captured and tortured a king's beloved mate and were in the process of killing him. The way I see it if I allow that to go unpunished, what's to stop someone from Rames or Dornte coming to Travon and seizing my future wife? Would I expect the man who did something so heinous to be punished? Yes, I would."

"And he would be," Creed says, dipping his chin. "Such a man would be executed on the spot. Made an example to send a message to all who think to use royals as leverage."

Satune nods. "Agreed."

"Let me do it," a woman says, stepping in behind Vikarus. The physical resemblance is unmistakable, and I realize this must be Rhy and Vik's mother. "Shadowcaster has wronged me more than any of you. Let me be the one to put him down."

The dragon alpha turns a furious gaze on the woman. As he does, she arches back and windmills her arms releasing two daggers.

End over end they fly with incredible speed and accuracy. One sinks into the center of his forehead and snaps his head back, so the other can pierce his throat.

There's a gruesome crack as his massive frame hits the rock wall and then he drops to the ground.

Vikarus grins and takes a knee. "All hail, Queen of the Dragon Clans, Aerial Silverwing."

Rhylan

I wake on my stomach with no idea where I am or what happened. Drawing a deep breath, my dragon surges to the fore and lets off a long growl. Sex. My mates' scents are all around me and considering how comfy I am, I'm in their mating bed.

"Finally, our sleeping dragon wakes." The mattress dips

beneath me as Keyla's scent grows stronger in my lungs. "Welcome home, Dragon. You've had us worried for a few hours."

A few hours?

I open my eyes, surprised the swelling has gone down enough to see her clearly. She's lying on her side next to me, her hair long and loose from the braid she normally wears, her expression soft and sweet.

"Slecking hell, you're beautiful."

She smiles, shifts closer, and runs a gentle touch across my cheek to move my hair out of my face. "Thank you."

"Are we good? Is it over? What did I miss?" I move to roll over and wince.

"Shhh, lay still," she says, urging me back to the mattress. "Calli's tears are amazing, but severe damage still takes time to heal."

I sink back into the silky comfort of Creed's sheets and let out a sigh. "Consider me convinced. I'd still like it if you bring me up to date. Are Creed and Dillan all right? Did you figure out that the witch was there? I think I tried to tell you, but I was pretty out of it. How did you even find me?"

Keyla goes on to tell me about how Creed's desperation to find me after Vik gave him the invitation, seems to have triggered their mating beacon and then, even though she was in the Human Realm, she felt the pull to get to me. "Calli and the quint joined in, and we brought Hawk's helicopter through the gate to Travon. Then we met up with Creed and his team for the battle at the lair."

I listen in amazement as she details my rescue and then how they tracked down the Blood Witch and how both the witch and Shadowcaster have been removed from the board.

"So, my mother is Queen of the Dragon Clans?"

"Yes. Her induction is today. I'm sorry to say you won't be in any shape to get there."

I shrug and groan as the pain of moving hits. "It doesn't

bother me to miss the ceremony. I belong here with Creed and you and Dillan. Even the Phoenix Quint have proven themselves more like family than my dragon brethren. After what they did to me, you guys are my only family now."

She snuggles closer, linking her arm with mine, and settles so we're nose-to-nose. "I'm glad you think so. I know it's strange at first, realizing that the family you're born to and the people who should love you most and have your back aren't always your forever family. I learned that when Kotah first mated with Calli. I think it's why I was so gung-ho to have you and Doc join me and Creed in our mating. I knew we could be the family we all needed."

"Creed told me your instincts are keen. You were ahead of us on that." My eyes are burning to close, but I don't want to lose this moment. "I'm sorry I fought it so hard. I almost died and missed out on the whole thing."

"What matters is that you didn't die." She leans forward and rubs noses with me. It's a playful act and my wildling side appreciates her wolf's presence. "All's well that ends well."

My eyes drift shut, and I fight to open them again.

She squeezes our joined hand and smiles. "Rest, Dragon. Your body needs time to recover."

My dragon growls and I force my eyes open for a moment longer. "Will you stay, Little Wolf? I feel a little floaty and I'm not ready to lose this connection. Neither is my dragon."

The joy dancing in those rich, brown eyes is the best medicine a guy could ask for. Lifting her chin, she brushes her lips against mine in a gentle show of affection. "Of course, sweetie. Close your eyes. I won't leave your side."

I hear the truth in her words, and I wonder why it took me so long to understand what it means.

We are mates.

CHAPTER SIXTEEN

Keyla

I spend the next few hours, lying next to Rhylan, easing his dragon while the man heals. Wildlings, like animals in the wild, respond badly to feeling vulnerable with others around, especially other males.

Since dragons are arguably the most dominant of the wildling species, it's my sole aim to ensure Rhylan's dragon never feels threatened.

The last thing we need is for him to lose control, shift, and crash through the bedroom wall. He needs to lay still while his wheals knit back together.

The bleeding and oozing has stopped and the swelling is going down by the hour but there are several puncture holes where daggers were thrust into him and left there that are slow to heal.

I think they will scar despite Calli's phoenix tears.

"That bad, is it?"

I lift my gaze from the diminishing damage and meet his

sleepy gaze. "Not bad, no. I was just thinking you won't get through this without at least a few scars."

He sighs, pain darkening his gaze. "I'll take the scars inflicted as part of my journey to get me here. The ones on the outside, at least. I'm not sure what to do with the scars on my insides."

I brush his stubbled cheek and cup his jaw. "I'm sorry you're hurting. If it helps, I understand what it's like to be judged and disappointed by a family who is supposed to love you."

He smiles, but I sense it is forced. "It helps."

Refusing to lose the physical contact of touching him, I brush my fingers along his temple and shift his hair out of his eyes so I can see him properly.

"I know you said before you think we should hold ourselves at a distance, but I'd like to revisit that. You were trying to spare me the trouble you thought you would bring—and I appreciate that—but you bring much more than trouble into my life."

A soft smile plays at the corner of his mouth, and it nurtures hope within me. "I don't know that I'm a strong enough male to resist you for any longer than I have. And yes, I said that for your sake... but if we're being honest there's also part of me afraid to invest in something that will truly damage me if torn away."

Aww, sweet male.

I slide my hand under the matted mass of his tangled blond hair and lean closer. Pressing my lips softly to his, I give him a moment to breathe in my sincerity and devotion to loving him. "I look forward to you being well enough to get up and about. There are things I'd like to do with you—well, *to* you, mostly— and I'd prefer for you not to wince through it."

A rush of arousal hits my nostrils and my wolf prowls forward, growling as she rises to the surface.

Rhylan's pupils flare. "Even after everything?"

"Of course. You are mine, Rhylan Silverwing. Mine to care

for, to worry over, to support, and to love. Creed chose you and loved you first, but I look forward to showing you he's not the only one for you."

"If you're serious about that..."

My wolf stretches inside me and lifts her head. "I am. What's on your mind?"

"Phoenix tears are great... but I'll heal better if I feed. If that's too much too soon, I understand but—"

I roll off the bed, my heart racing. Feed him?

When his brows come down, I smile and pull my top over my head. After that's gone, I shove my pants down and shed my panties and socks. I practically launch back onto the mattress.

So much for playing hard to get.

Lifting the covers, I snuggle in next to him, lift my head, and gather my hair out of his way. "Ready when you are."

Warm breath tickles my throat as he rises and props up on his elbow. "That eager, are you?"

I picture him pinning Creed up against the wall and a rush of moisture slicks my core. "You've taken Creed's and Dillan's vein. I want that too. Take what I offer freely, to heal you and complete our bond."

He studies my expression and I know he's looking for any sign that I'm not sure—but I *am* sure.

When he finds no hesitation, he meets my gaze. "The initial strike will sting, but my saliva will quickly replace the pain with an almost drugged pleasure."

"I saw and felt that when you drank from Creed. Don't worry about me. I've thought a lot about this." Actually, thinking about it now has me scissoring my legs, aching to get started.

Rhy breathes deeply and his half-masted eyes flash gold. His wild side is pressing forward, his dragon eager to claim what is his. "And the sexual component? Have you considered that as well?"

Between the scent of his arousal and the energy of his dragon vibrating across our mental connection, he has me keyed up and randy. The throbbing between my legs is getting hard to ignore.

"Yes. I offer you *all* of me, to use and consume as you need. I am yours as you are mine."

He shakes his head and sighs. "You're far too trusting, Little Wolf."

I tilt my head away, giving him full access to my neck. "Take from me or don't, but don't tell me what I want or what I can handle."

The deep-throated chuckle brings his chest to mine and he slides over me. "Creed warned me you aren't like females of this realm. All right. If you're sure, I will happily take your vein and bury myself in your lush heat."

I open my thighs and make room for him to shift over me fully. He's heavier than Creed but not as heavy as Doc, and when the cradle of his hips rest at the crux of my body I think of Goldilocks and smile.

Not too heavy. Not too light.

He's juuust right.

He settles into place, the head of his cock nudging my entrance. Sexual energy zings through me, calling my release, and tightening in my womb.

Damn. I might come before we even get started.

Rhylan nuzzles against the pulse of blood pounding in my veins and my wolf lets off a howl. The anticipation is killing me. I'm practically panting for him.

"Do it." I swallow but my mouth remains dry. "Drink from me. Fuck me. Claim me as your own."

His dragon growls and then he drops his head.

He draws his tongue up the column of my throat and I swallow against his tongue.

Can people die from anticipation?

If so, I'm in real danger of dropping dead.

The strike is fast and brutal. I cry out, stiffening as his canines pierce my flesh and puncture my jugular.

My wolf instincts flare as he latches onto my throat. My mind wars over my body as I lock my reflexes, fighting not to push him away.

And then, everything changes.

In the next beat of my racing heart, the momentary panic and pain subsides, replaced by a wave of pleasure. I groan. My body relaxes. I release the breath locked in my lungs. "Oh, yes."

Rhylan adjusts his lips against my throat and suckles and pulls. The process makes my nipples and my inner muscles ache with need. "I need you inside me. Please."

Rhylan adjusts his upper body, pressing forward to circle his hips and slick his cock. The sweeping of his engorged tip through the moisture he's called from me is magical and I have to focus on breathing to fend off a round of dizziness.

The penetration is invasive, and it takes a moment for him to sink fully into my depths.

Yes, I'm new to sex and tight—Doc and Creed have both mentioned that—but Rhylan is also a sizable male.

I'm careful where I set my hands on his shoulders, very aware the skin on his back and ass and thighs is a roadmap of abuse and violence.

His dragon's energy is strong, and my wolf appreciates his dominance. He has wanted to assert his claim on me for days and now, at last, the beast revels in the triumph of a true mating.

Rhylan growls as he starts a slow push and retreat. His presence inside me stretches my limits in the most delicious ways. He's almost too much, but at the same time, not enough—never enough.

I groan and rock my hips. "Don't be polite. I need your hunger. I want you uncensored. Don't hurt yourself, but don't hold back on my account."

Locked inside me as deeply as he can go, his body shudders, and then his hips start to pump in earnest.

Creed

Dillan and I take in the erotic show, and I can't help but think Keyla is giving Rhylan the kind of healing he truly needs. Sure, the phoenix tears and blood will help, but Rhylan's deepest wounds come from what was done to him by his family and friends.

Keyla's unconditional acceptance and soothing ways will ease those wounds—I know from experience.

Rhylan's hips rock in a slow and steady rhythm of in and out and Keyla arches against the mattress beneath him. His head is bent, his mouth sealed against the silky column of her neck.

I remember the sensation well from his claiming of me. My body surges behind the fabric of my pants and I reach down to adjust things.

Fuck that's hot, Dillan says into my mind.

I couldn't agree more. *I say we take our time in joining them. After Rhy's fed and is feeling stronger, we'll welcome him into our foursome properly.*

I like the way you think, mate. Dillan pulls his shirt off over his head and starts unbuckling his belt.

As he strikes off toward the washroom, I unbutton my shirt, discard my pants, and take a seat in the reading chair in view of the bed.

Not wanting to disturb the feeding, I grip my length and tug at it. I'm an independent male. I can service myself until there's a break in the action.

Closing my eyes, I tap into the mental energy of the room,

and my cock jumps in my grip. Yeah. Living with these three will feed my need for powerful mental connections for years to come.

And feed my soul too.

Keyla cries out, her body arching against Rhylan's steady thrust and retreat. As her first orgasm hits, her heels dig into the mattress, and she shatters beneath him.

Fuck. I nearly come just watching them.

Rhy finishes with his feeding, but he isn't finished fucking her. He lifts onto his palms and rides out her orgasm with style. When the intensity of her release settles, Rhy glances over his shoulder. "Are you two going to amuse yourselves with a rub and tug in the shadows all night or are you planning on joining us?"

I get my naked ass in gear and take him up on the invitation. "We were being gentlemen, giving you two a moment to yourselves."

"There are more orifices to fill," Rhy says. "I'm quite happy where I am, but I think Doc should give Keyla something to suck on and Creed, you know where I want you."

I chuckle and grab the bottle of lubrication and a string of cock sheaths from the bedside drawer. "Feeling better, I take it."

Rhylan is a machine.

I've never seen him with a female, but I know how he is with me. He's dominant and insatiable. He bent to my will in the past, but I think now that we're mated, and our relationship is somewhat out in the open, my days of calling all the shots are coming to an end.

Doc climbs onto the bed and brushes a finger over the side of Keyla's neck. "Hey, babe. How you doing?"

"Good," she says, her voice strained. "I think you were told to give me something to suck on."

The bear lets off a rolling laugh and crawls across the top of the bed to settle over her on his hands and knees. "Yes, my queen."

I laugh too.

This new life of ours is something else.

Growing up, my father stressed the importance of humility. A king shouldn't laud himself over others or he would alienate his people.

Here, like this with them, I totally get off on the rush of being in control. Squeezing a glob of liquid into my palm, I crawl in behind Rhy's toned and beautiful ass. "And I was told to take up the rear."

The growl of Rhylan's dragon triggers a burst of tingling in my sac. *Fuck.* How lost in denial was I to not realize he affects me as deeply as he does?

I take in the damage to Rhylan's body and if Shadowcaster wasn't already dead, I'd kill him again.

Don't let them take anything more from us, Keyla says, meeting my gaze. *Stay in the present. The wounds will heal.*

I nod and get my mind back on track.

Even red and welted, Rhylan is a beautifully built male. Focusing on pleasuring him, I slick things up and play, stretching him and getting him ready for what's to come. I've taken him rough and angry so many times.

Not this time.

Maybe never again.

Squaring my hips behind him, I slip on a sheath and press the tip of my cock against the restriction of his ass. It's crazy but doing this with Keyla and Dillan here is a touch unnerving. Rhylan and I have always been dark and dirty. Now we're in love.

It's a strange new reality.

"Slecking hell, Creed, hurry up," Rhy snaps. "I'm dying here."

"Hush and be patient. You've had enough rough for a day or two. Let me give you a little loving care." I take another squirt of lubrication and give my cock a couple of priming strokes. Without fanfare, I press my swollen tip where I want to be and push past the resistance blocking me from my pleasure.

Our pleasure.

Rhylan lets off a groan as I push deeper. Having been on the receiving end of this before, I know how it burns at first. No mercy though.

Rhylan loves the burn.

After a couple of strong strokes, I'm slicked up and set a pace. The skin on Rhy's hips is almost fully healed, so I grip the bones of his physique and use the leverage to pump.

He bucks beneath me and Keyla shudders beneath him. She's got her mouth full, sucking Dillan off. When I put real force into my thrusts, her knees open wider.

I chuckle as she lifts her legs in the air, spreading wider for us. Gripping her calves, I pull her to leverage my thrusts. Rhylan rams into her as I ram into him and she's pinned in place.

The forward thrust has my balls slapping against his and it's so good. "How rough do you guys want this?" I ask, my heart pounding in my chest.

Keyla's wolf growls and she opens up the connection in our minds, sending me images of me fucking them senseless. I'm not surprised. She likes to start wild and end with loving and sensitive.

That's fine with me.

Rhy's dragon surges forward and he's all wildling and carnal pleasure.

"Punishing and pounding, it is." I set caution to the side and build momentum until I'm pounding home and my lungs burn with the exertion.

The thundering *slap, slap, slap* of flesh echos in the air, and each time I slam home, Keyla lets off a feminine grunt of pleasure. The bear growls and my release burns hot in my balls.

Yeah, Bear, your turn is coming.

I say we do this all night long, Keyla gasps.

We're going to be sore tomorrow, I say.

Worth it, Rhy says, pushing back against my hips.

Fuck I love the wild side Rhylan calls forward.

I love getting rough with him. I'd never been with a guy before him, but when locked behind closed doors you gotta improvise and go with what you've got.

Who knew it would turn out like this?

Rhy groans and, connected as we are, I feel how hard he's fighting his release. He's trying to lock down he's losing the fight.

"How good is it, Rhy?"

"You're hitting me so hard and deep... my god."

I bark a laugh. "Are you saying I am your god? Do you worship me, Dragon?"

"Right now, yes." His fists grip the mattress, his shoulders bulging with the strain of bracing himself against my thrusts. "You're a slecking god."

Yeah, I am.

But I don't forget about the other two.

Keyla is too sexy. Her hair is wild, her cheeks flushed as they hollow and fill as she sucks Doc's cock. And then there are her breasts. Round and firm, they jostle and bounce with each thrust Rhy and I fill her with.

Stunning.

And then there's Dillan.

Our bear is framed with a mass of bulk and strength and with his dark features and those piercing hazel eyes, he's heart-stoppingly sexy. He's got his hips locked and is fighting his urge to fuck Keyla's mouth and the excruciating pleasure on his face is too much.

I never knew I was into guys, but now that I'm mated to two of them—yeah, I so am.

Sweat drips from my brow and I adjust my grip from Keyla's legs to Rhy's hips. Fucking like a god is a full-bodied workout.

Over the past couple of years with Rhy, I learned he is both addictive and tireless.

But even with as many orgasms as we have shared, we never crossed the line into affection. The emotional connection tonight raises everything to a new level.

Everything is just... more.

The air rings with the sounds of sex, of four bodies slapping, throaty gasps, and wildling growls.

It's fucking amazing.

Man, I could torture them like this all night long and by the mental energy I'm getting, they'd let me. But they have ideas and wants too, and I won't steal the show.

"All right. Let's end round one with a bang and give someone else control. Brace yourselves. I'm going hard and then you can show me what you've got."

The next few minutes are an explosion of body slapping and throaty grunts. The carnal pleasures take us to the precipice and then Keyla cries out and comes undone. Her hips buck, her body undulating in graceful lines and rounded curves.

She's barely finished when Doc curses and locks his hips. Keyla's wolf growls and then she's swallowing everything he's giving her.

Rhylan is next. His head comes back, and he thrusts his cock hard, locking his hips. The dark spice of his mating scent explodes into the air, and I realize by the end of this, we will all be wearing that scent.

His ass clenches and my cock is gripped so tight, I can't hold off.

Too. Fucking. Much.

I thrust hard and join them in the release of my lifetime. Hot jets of cream let loose, and my eyes roll back. After he's thoroughly marked and everyone is panting and gasping for breath, I collapse onto his sweaty back.

Reaching around, I plant my palms on the bed next to Keyla's ribs to keep from collapsing and crushing them. Rhylan's body is heaving almost as hard as mine as I nuzzle into the back of his hair. "So, this is us. Welcome to the mating, Dragon."

Rhy barks a laugh. "If that was the demonstration of what's to come, consider me all-in."

CHAPTER SEVENTEEN

Keyla

𝒯he four of us lockdown for the next two days, leaving the suite as little as possible. Between the physical damage done to Rhylan to the emotional wounds inflicted because of Bloom's suffering, we all need time to heal and solidify our bonds.

But, in the end, nothing can hold back the needs of the quadrant.

Creed and I are the royal leaders of Dornte and as my father always said, 'A leader must embrace his duty—despite personal sentiment, obstacles, dangers, or pressures from others. To fail in this is to lose the honor of being a male of worth.'

As a child, I found his constant drilling exhausting.

Now that I'm in a position of rule, his words manifest in my mind at moments when I need them most.

It makes my wolf howl to know the loss of him was calculated and senseless, but I'm trying to focus on what I gained from him instead of what I lost.

"Hey, mates," Dillan says, catching up with Creed and me

outside the throne room. "How are the interviews going? Found any traitors yet?"

I step into his embrace and reach up to kiss his cheek. "No. Everyone has been so supportive and many of them have constructive ideas about how to re-establish Dornte as a power in the realm."

Creed chuckles, casting me an adoring glance. "That's because we made it clear that anyone not on team Thornebane needed to vacate the quadrant. The only people left are our supporters."

I shrug. "It has still been a good morning, filled with positive energy."

Creed smiles at Dillan and the two of them seem to share a private conversation that I'm not part of.

"What?" I say, frowning. "Did I say something?"

"Nothing to warrant that look of concern," Creed says. "Dillan and I were speaking this morning about what a blessing you are to a weary soul. Your optimism and uplifting attitude make it easy to forget the worries and strife which befalls us on a regular basis."

Doc winks at me. "Don't get your ruff riled, babe. S'all good. We were speaking your praises, promise."

I smile and feel my cheeks flush warm. "Well, that's lovely, thank you."

The three of us fall into step and make our way through the corridors back to the suite. Over the past couple of days, we've been walking the halls a great deal to allow the staff and visitors around the castle to get used to seeing us together.

Usually, Rhy is with us, but he had a personal errand to take care of outside the castle, so we're a man down today.

"How are things with Isabo, babe?" Doc asks. "Do you think you're going to like working with her?"

"I do. She knows the ins and outs of the role of the Dornte queen yet she's open to allowing me to make my own decisions.

She guided life behind the scenes, helping Creed's mother run the castle and staff but doesn't seem territorial about me asserting myself. From what I've seen so far, I think we'll work well together."

"I'm glad to hear that," Creed says. "My mother adored the woman. I was hoping it might work out between you two."

The two men standing guard at the doors to the heirs' corridor bow their heads and open the doors for us as we pass.

"Thank you, gentlemen," I say, offering them a kind smile. "Blessed be."

Creed chuckles. "You are so incredibly polite."

I shrug. "Why wouldn't I be? I know how it feels to have people ignore me and dismiss my importance. I won't ever do that to others."

"No. Of course, you won't."

Doc steps ahead of us as we arrive at our suite and presses his hand over the security scanner to access the heirs' suite. Inside, we find Kotah and the guys sitting on the two couches and pouring over paperwork spread out on the stone coffee table between them.

"What are we working on today?" I ask, waving my hands to have them sit back down.

It's weird when they jump to their feet every time I come into a room. They are my brothers-in-law for goodness sake, not my subjects.

Kotah stands and stretches. "Hawk's courier came through the gate a couple of hours ago and brought us the findings on Raven and what she has been up to."

I step over to have a look. "Is it all phone records?"

Hawk tilts his head from side to side. "Mostly. It would be difficult to find much more so after the fact. We'll keep digging, but you can learn a lot from phone records."

"And what have we learned?"

"She lived pretty much cut off from Hunter and my father

but there's a pattern to the calls. There are the weekly check-in calls, which are longer and presumably a chance for husband and wife to stay in touch, and the quick update calls that seem to correspond with other events that occurred in the realm and our lives."

I look at the sheets of dates and numbers and frown. "Other events such as what?"

Kotah lifts a shoulder. "Mostly things we already suspected. We know for a fact she was the one giving away our position during Calli's quest. We confirmed she spoke to Hunter when we first arrived at the castle and the day the helicopter raided our rental home outside Seattle when Calli was kidnapped."

"When Raven and Mother showed up out of nowhere and crashed our party right before we were invaded."

Brant nods. "We got lucky that when she escaped, she landed in that farmer's field in my sleuth's home territory and one of my bear brothers found her."

I point my thumb toward Honor's door. "Is she in there?"

Kotah nods. "She's keeping Honor company as Lukas works to remove the damage done by the Blood Witch."

Yuck. Even the mention of her brings images to mind of Creed causing her head to literally explode.

That was messy business.

"Lukas has gone over and above," Creed says. "I don't know how I'll ever be able to repay him."

I don't so much hear Creed's discomfort but feel it in the air. We haven't figured out if my powers are me manifesting his mind guardian abilities or my abilities taking form or a combination of the two, but sensing mental energies is becoming easier for me.

"What is it?" I ask, searching the strain of his expression.

He hugs me to his side and whispers into my ear. "It's nothing, Little Wolf. I'm fine."

It's both amusing and annoying that he thinks he can get

away with comments like that. *I smell your pain. Please tell me what's wrong. I'd like to help if I can.*

"How are the coronation plans going?" Jaxx asks.

Creed takes the change of subject and heads over to the bar. "Everything seems to be in order. The traditions of the ceremony were established four generations ago, so it's simply a matter of having it and broadcasting it to the quadrant."

"He's already the king anyway," Doc says.

"And a popular one at that," I say, watching him to see if I can discern what's bothering him. "With our abolishment of the nightly curfews and the reinstatement of public programs, the citizens of Dornte are happy to have him in power."

Brant chuffs. "It's not hard to raise the bar from Laryssa's brutal insanity. The citizens of Dornte are glad to see the end of a narcissistic dictator in power." He sends Creed an apologetic smile. "And I'm sure you're rocking it too."

Creed waves that away. "No need to apologize. You aren't wrong. Anyone is better than Laryssa."

I scoff. "That's not true. You're the king Dornte needs and when the citizens see our plans and how we run things, they will love you even more."

Watching Creed as I am, I see his wince as he raises his glass to swallow his drink. "We'll leave you to your sleuthing. The three of us are going to freshen up and then go down to the castle dining hall for something to eat. All those who would like to join, are welcome."

Brant chuckles. "I'll never turn down food."

"We won't be long."

Doc eyes me up, but when I gesture for him to head into our bedroom, he doesn't argue. Creed hesitates, but without making a scene, there's no getting out of it.

The three of us step inside our bedroom and I close the door. "Now, what is it you're not saying. Why are you in so much pain?"

"It has something to do with the scars on your back, doesn't it?" Doc says, his voice deep and graveled. "I know you don't like to talk about them, but you gotta be straight with us."

"I'll be fine."

"I'm sure you will," he says, "but if Keyla was in pain and wouldn't tell us what hurt or why, you'd lose your mind, right? This is no different."

~

Creed

Wildlings can smell the scent of a lie as well as the scent of my discomfort, so there's no point in denying it. I'm not sure why I'm even reluctant to tell them. They are my mates. They have seen the scars. At some point soon they will realize I no longer have my wings.

I draw a deep breath and try to find the words to express my deepest humiliation. I walk deeper into our bedroom and lean against the footboard of our bed. "One of the first things Laryssa and the Blood Witch did to ensure I would remain their prisoner was to try to break me and ensure I could neither fight back nor fly away."

Dillan's bear is already growling.

"The witch blocked my powers, she cursed me with the beast, but the most damaging thing she did to me was slice off my faery wings."

Dillan's mental anguish is filled with hostility and anger. He confided in me once that he too has a physical deficiency due to violence beyond his control.

Keyla's response, however, is heartbreak. "I'm so sorry, my prince."

I sigh. "Sometimes they ache deep inside my back. There's

nothing to be done about it and I prefer not to talk about it. What is a faery without wings?"

"I can't speak for all faeries," Keyla says, "but in your case, he is a male of worth, a mate, a lover, a friend, and a strong leader. He is a king of men."

Doc nods. "She's right. What's done is done. People don't come out of wars unscathed. Sometimes the wounds are visible, sometimes not, but they all add to the person we move on to be."

Keyla steps close and wraps her arms around my waist, laying her cheek on my chest. "Is there anything we can do to help with the pain?"

"There's a bottle of pain liniment in my cabinet that helps a lot. I've been too ashamed to talk about it, so haven't asked if one of you might help me with it."

Dillan strides around the bed and goes into the bathroom. "Blue bottle with a white lid?"

"That's it."

Our bear returns and Keyla eases back. With gentle care, she pops each button of my shirt free from its mooring and then steps back. "Take off your shirt and then lay on your stomach."

I do as she says and a moment later, she climbs up onto the bed and straddles my ass. "Don't keep things from us. We are your mates. There is nothing you can't share—nothing we won't understand and support you through. We love you."

"One of the hardest parts of being a bear is realizing that no matter how big and strong you feel, there are some things you can't handle on your own. Asking for help, whether it be for something physical or emotional, doesn't make you weaker, it makes you stronger."

I hear what he's saying but when Keyla slicks her hands and kneads at the ache, nothing else registers.

The relief is exquisite.

After hours of agony to not have the pain is heaven. "This is how Rhylan and I started up back at the beginning of things. He smelled my pain and would come in at night to check on me. Eventually, I accepted his help."

"And one thing led to another and eventually you accepted more of him than that," Dillan says.

I chuckle. "I suppose that's true."

Keyla rubs over the scars and the sliced muscles, bone, and nerve-endings beneath my skin finally relent. "I will do this for as long as you need and as often as you want, my love."

I let out a long sigh of relief. "You better not offer yourself up for as long as I want. I may never let you leave this bed."

She leans forward, sweeps my hair to one side, and brushes her lips against my neck. "Easing your suffering is my honor as your mate. Please don't shut us out. Trust me with the bad in your life as well as the good."

I glance over my shoulder at her and draw a deep, breath. "I trust you, Little Wolf. More than I thought possible."

CHAPTER EIGHTEEN

Rhylan

There's a Human Realm saying, *If you want change, you have to invite chaos.* Having been Laryssa's muscle for two years, I think the people of Dornte have suffered through enough chaos, but I see the wisdom in those words. There's another saying too, *Be the change you wish to see in the world.*

These two principles have kept me busy over the past week as we settle in and the quadrant adjusts to falling, once again, under Thornebane rule.

Creed and Keyla are doing everything right. They are leading Dornte through a transition from a troubled time with strength and compassion. The majority of citizens respect that and are hopeful for what is to come.

There are a great many powerful people who don't.

One of the reasons Laryssa's wave of power washed to shore with such strength was because she had money and corruption behind her. To cut off the head of the snake is not enough.

Weeding out the evils rooted and woven into the fabric of our society is necessary.

And as much as I despise it, I'm seen as part of Laryssa's camp. Most people can't tell Vik and me apart, so, with that in mind, I've been visiting some of the figureheads I know Laryssa dealt with.

This isn't as over as Creed and Keyla hope it is.

I don't want to be an alarmist, but Dornte has troubled times ahead. I don't want to let our happiness cloud our vision of what might be coming at us. Normally, this would be handled by the Guardian of the Crown, which is Honor, but she's still comatose.

"There you are," Creed says, catching me coming out of the Dornte War Room.

I watch him stride down the corridor toward me, his long, silver hair flowing behind those broad shoulders and my breath tightens in my chest.

Too slecking hot.

"What are you doing down here?"

"I figured with Honor unable to resume her place at the helm of Dornte security right now, I'd keep an eye on things and assess the state of the quadrant in the aftermath of Laryssa's removal from office."

Creed nods. "And? Where do things stand?"

"Overall, we're in good shape."

"The citizens seem happy."

I press my hand to the security screen and take him back inside to show him what I've been working on the past three days. Typing in my passcodes, I bring the war table online and call my research forward. "The majority of the citizens are, yes, but Laryssa had five primary supporters and more who supported her because she leveraged their self-interests. Simply because she's gone, doesn't mean their goals to rise to power within the quadrant will diminish."

Creed frowns. "No. I wouldn't expect so. I'm disappointed, though. My father considered some of these men friends."

As he assesses who I've targeted and why, I pull up another

array of photos. "The ones I marked with red tabs have actively worked to undermine you. I witnessed them plotting with Laryssa myself. The ones tagged in orange are people I know of from second-hand conversations with Laryssa or Vik."

"And the ones tagged green?"

"Those are people Laryssa placed on her watch list because they were too loyal to the Thornebanes for their own good."

"It's nice to know someone was loyal to my family."

"By my estimation, ninety-five percent of Dornte citizens support a Thornebane reign. And if the other five percent don't want to get on board, they can leave. There are other quadrants they can live in."

"Rames would be good. Let them take on the Golden Army and then see how rebellious they feel."

"Exactly."

When he turns from the table, he steps close and brushes my hair back to see my face. "Thank you for being here for me—for choosing me even when it cost you so much."

"Talk about being disappointed in a lack of loyalty. I never expected to be thrown away by my mother and my twin. I don't even know what to do with that."

He advances, easing me back so my ass bumps the table behind me and he pins me in place. Leaning in, he brushes his mouth over mine and nips my bottom lip. "Do with it whatever you need to. In the grand scheme of things, it doesn't matter. We love you. *I* love you."

I know he does, but it's nice to hear—especially with the scent of his affection filling my senses. I swallow, wanting more of his mouth. "Kiss me again."

He does. Pelvis-to-pelvis, chest-to-chest, mouth-to-mouth we spend the next few minutes kissing one another in passionate sweeps of tongues and lips.

When he pulls back, he's as breathless as I am.

He glances at my lips and the hunger in those ebony eyes is

the sexiest thing ever. "I understand that our coming together was a whirlwind of hostility and bitterness. We never got soft and sexy with one another, but I want you to hear me say it and know I mean it. I love you."

I nod. "Thank you for including me in your marriage. Thank you for not leaving me behind."

He frowns. "Leave you behind? You stood by me when my life was only pain and betrayal. You are the *one* person who gave a shit about me for two long, lonely years. Keyla may have seen it first, but I would've gotten there. You have to be with us because you own a piece of my heart. I'm not whole without you."

I'm at a loss for words, but thankfully, a notification pings on Creed's datapad. He eases back and smiles as he reads the screen. "Wonderful."

I grin. "What's wonderful?"

"I have a surprise for us." He taps for the keyboard screen and starts swiping through the letters to send a message. When he hits send, there is another ping almost immediately afterward. "I have something to check on first and I've asked Keyla and Doc to meet us at the eternal tree in thirty minutes. Does that work for you?"

I close my files and shut down the war table. "It might be tight, but I won't be much longer. I have something I want to take care of as well. I'll meet you there."

Keyla

Doc and I walk together through the public areas of the castle and I smile at the onlookers. Many of the faces are becoming familiar to me and I'm pleased to smell their growing affection. They're getting used to seeing the four of us together and once they realized that Creed and I are the ruling couple, they seem to have stopped caring about four people in our marriage altogether.

As horrible as it is to think, Laryssa being a vile bitch has made people very welcoming to Creed and me.

"So, any hints as to what Creed's surprise is about?" Doc asks.

"Not that he mentioned, no. He asked us to meet him at the entrance to the royal residence wing near the statue of the bronze tree in twenty minutes."

I gesture to the tree ahead and smile at Creed arriving from a different direction. Then I see Creed's attention shift to another corridor converging from a third direction and I squeal like a teenager—

"Oh, my goodness. Look at you."

I rush to close the distance and raise my hands to Rhylan's face. The long, sweep of hair that has hidden his face and eyes from the world is gone and his beautiful turquoise eyes are shining out at us like two gorgeous tropical pools. "Sweet Powers, you're so beautiful."

Creed chuckles behind me and lifts his hand to stroke over the short, shaved sides of his head. The top is still shaggy and long, but now it's chic instead of a mop. "Men prefer words like handsome or hot."

"Hot definitely works," Doc says, stepping in to join the admiration. "Fuck, Dragon, you're rockin' my cock like crazy. This look suits you."

The side of Rhy's mouth quirks up in a shy grin. "Thanks. I figured—new man, new life, new look."

"I vote we use one of these alcoves and show you how much we like the new look," I say, eyeing the closest hidden nook.

Creed chuckles. "I like where you're going with that, Little Wolf, but let's finish with my surprise first. It might segue into your idea."

I grin. "Alrighty, I'm even more curious now. What is this wonderous surprise you're planning?"

Doc nods. "Does it have to do with your coronation ceremony tomorrow? Your sister? Something Lukas learned from going through the Blood Witch's condo?"

Creed smiles. "All good guesses, Bear, but no."

I giggle. "Then his guesses weren't that good."

Doc laughs. "Good point."

"Follow me and all will be revealed."

Creed leads us through the upper levels of the castle to a large set of double doors on the main floor. The wide archway curls between two massive stone columns that hold two heavy, iron-studded doors.

I glanced up at the spiked metal portcullis suspended in their brackets above our heads and wince. The tips are sharpened to pierce and impale those passing beneath. "This entrance is very imposing. Where are we going?"

Creed glances up at the threatening metal grates. "This is the public division between the King's quarters in the north wing and all the rooms related to realm business. These gates separate the two and, as well as being dropped at night, can also be dropped and locked from either side if anything dangerous happens in the course of our duties."

Our duties. I love the sound of that. Growing up the daughter of the Fae Prime, it was apparent that despite my natural disposition to realm politics and aptitude for ruling, I'd never be more than the sister of the Prime.

Kotah had every intention of integrating me into his reign, but it would never have been mine to claim.

Dornte is *mine.*

Creed and I will rule this quadrant together and I couldn't be happier. There's nothing I need... except maybe one thing.

I glance at my empty fingers and frown. "Is there a Queen's

ring in this realm? Not that I need one, but I grew up admiring my mother's ring and always dreamed of wearing one."

Creed nods. "When the invasion began, my father had all the priceless symbols of our family gathered and sealed away. Laryssa never found them, and I requested them retrieved a couple of days ago. You are welcome to look through what's there and are free to claim whatever you wish."

"After I speak to Honor, of course," I say. "She should have the first pick when it comes to your mother's jewelry."

Creed's silver brows arch. "As the Queen of Dornte, *you* are the true and rightful owner of everything in the Queen's collection. There are other items that are considered family treasures which Honor will claim as the Thornebane daughter and Guardian of the Crown, but honestly, my sister is more warrior than a princess. Don't hold back on her account."

I hear what he's saying but still think Honor should have first dibs.

We breach the threshold that marks the division between the public castle and what Creed described as the king's wing.

The heels of my new thigh-high leather boots beat out a solid, surefooted rhythm as we move across the glass sheen of the granite floor. The boys haven't seen them yet, but Dillan and Creed fantasized once, and I am looking forward to surprising them.

The corridors become quieter, the further we go into the space, and I slip my hand into the crook of the elbows of my dark prince and my beloved bear. If I had another side and another arm, I'd add Rhylan in too, but he seems content at Creed's side.

I draw a deep breath into my lungs and smile. Doc smells like sunshine and evergreens, Creed like freshly laundered dress clothes and leather, and Rhylan like night skies and autumn breezes.

I breathe their scents deep into my lungs and smile at how things have changed.

We all have the same underlying scent but overtaking that is the blended influences of our mating. The four of us have spent enough time naked over the past days to make it very clear to anyone we come in contact with that we are very much claimed.

Which is rather wonderful.

I've never been a jealous or possessive female but eliminating any chance of confusion as to the fact that these men belong to me keeps everyone happy... and all limbs attached.

Creed kisses the side of my head and squeezes me to his side. "Why is your wolf growling?"

I blink and shake myself inwardly. "Sorry, I was just reveling in the claims we've made and thinking about what I'd be capable of if some ambitious beauty thought to step in on one of you."

Dillan chuckles. "By the sound of your wolf's warning, you were envisioning gnawing off limbs and ripping out throats."

I grin wide and bite my teeth together. "You're exactly right, Bear. It's good you know what's in store."

"I like a girl with bite," Rhylan says winking at me. "Let me know if you ever have an insatiable urge to nip on something."

"Rhy, I have an insatiable urge to nip on something," I say without missing a beat.

Creed chuckles. "I can't take you three anywhere."

"You could take us back to our suite," Doc suggests. "Problem solved."

"Patience, mates. You can get naked where we're going, but not until I've shown you my surprise."

I chuckle. "Well then, why didn't you say so. Lead the way King Thornebane."

Creed

King Thornebane... she's hilarious. Keyla and I have spent the past two days together, sorting through the castle staff, reading and discussing comments, and getting her accustomed to Dornte traditions. The work has been relatively boring and tedious.

They've been the best days of my life.

When we get to where we're going, I stop and nod to the goblin male standing sentry. "Majesty, I wasn't certain if you'd need help keying in the security scans for your mates." He glances at Rhylan and drops his gaze. "Apologies... I didn't realize... of course, you're in capable hands."

I sense his anxiety, but it's much more about not wanting to make a misstep than it is about Rhylan himself. "I will announce it at my coronation tomorrow, but to be clear, Keyla Northwood and I are the royal couple and Dillan Baskins and Rhylan Silverwing are our beloved mates. We four are one in all things."

The male nods. "Of course, Majesty. I simply wasn't thinking."

I pat his shoulder. "This is an exciting time. Let us embrace new ideas."

"Yes, Majesty," he says, stepping away from the door. "Do you need anything more from me?"

"No. You are free to resume your duties."

"Thank you for thinking of us," Keyla says, reaching forward to squeeze his arm. "Blessed be."

When the corridor is empty except for the four of us, I gesture to the security screen and step aside to let Rhylan in. He taps a few things into the pad and then presses my hand against the screen. After my palm is scanned, he repeats the process with Keyla, Dillan, and then himself.

"What is the password to lock out changes to these permissions?"

I look at Keyla and smile. "Quadruple. Since Keyla made it up, it's the perfect password"

Keyla laughs. "I did not make that up."

"Of course, you did."

"It's a real word. Tell him, Bear."

Dillan looks at me and grins. "She's not wrong. It's a normal word, she just changed the pronunciation to fit our situation. It's pronounced quadroople. When she talks about us as a four-person couple, she says it her own way."

"Well, it's still my pick for a password."

"Add your security digits too," Keyla suggests. "That would add a level of difficulty."

Rhylan nods and types it in.

"And now that we're finished with that, can we see our surprise?" Keyla asks.

Rhylan draws a deep breath and chuckles. "Our Little Wolf is giving off distinct mating vibes."

Now it's my turn to laugh. "I promised a happy ending but I also said you need to be patient."

Rhylan's brow arches and it's wonderful to see his face unhindered. "Patience seems to be in short supply. Let's not keep the lady waiting."

Pressing my hand over the scanner, the ID screening beeps and allows me access. "Welcome to the King's Tower," I say, stepping inside and gesturing for them to follow. The massive rotunda inside the main entrance is decorated in charcoal gray and silver with pale blue, velvet drapes, and a silver-gilt dome high above. "These will be our living quarters from now on."

Doc

"Holy shitters. This place is unbelievable." I step away from Keyla and Creed to have a peek into the main rooms. "Wow. Look at this bar." I stride across the polished stone floor and around the two oversized couches by the fireplace. The bar on the far wall is fifteen feet long and stocked with glass shelves backlit to practically glow. "Jaxx will lose his mind."

"He will," Keyla says, turning to take it all in. "Oh, look at that view."

"Dornte at night has always taken my breath away," Creed says.

"That's because it's beautiful."

He smiles, taking her hand. "Come. There's more I want you to see."

He gives us the tour of two receiving rooms, a games room, and the exercise room and then points at a closed door. "Doc, I think you'll like this room."

I arch a brow and Keyla grins and moves aside so that I can take the lead. Opening things up, I swing the two massive doors out of our way and my jaw drops.

With fifteen-foot ceilings and shelves lining every wall my brain shorts out. "Unbelievable. How many books are in here?"

Creed shrugs. "I have no idea but if you want, you can count them. I know how much you love to read, I thought you might enjoy losing yourself in here. There is fiction and non-fiction and historical accounts and pretty much anything you might be interested in."

"I can hardly wait to dive in."

"Me too," Keyla says. "There's so much about StoneHaven and Dornte and the Wars of Power I want to learn about."

"And Kotah," I say, brushing my fingers down some of the spines. "He's our Rhodes Scholar."

Keyla chuckles. "He may never return to rule his realm."

"And this is only the beginning." Creed points back out toward the hall and we follow him up an open staircase to a second story. If I'm not mistaken, he's having as much fun showing us our new quarters as we're having exploring them.

The study has two large desks with computers and leather

chairs—one considerably smaller than the other and built for the frame of a woman. "Is this our office?"

Creed nods. "My parents ruled together, and we shall do the same. You are my partner in all things. I'm thankful the universe chose you because I never would've gotten it so right."

"You say the sweetest things." Keyla pushes him against the desk for a long, slow kiss. When she palms the front of his slacks and he arches his hips into her hold the study is suddenly filled with a wave of sexual promise.

"Are we christening this room or continuing the tour?" I untuck my shirt to give myself a little extra space in my pants.

"Christening what?" Creed asks. "What does that mean, Bear?"

I arch a brow. "It's customary in our realm that when you get a new home, a young couple or newly married couple has sex in each of the rooms to make the space their own. You know... for good luck. To bless you in the life to come."

Rhylan chokes out a laugh. "There are a lot of rooms in the King's Tower. We are going to be very busy for a very long time."

Creed nods. "Is there a deadline on how much time we have to get this christening complete?"

Keyla laughs. "No, silly. It's just for fun."

"Oh, it's going to be fun," Rhylan says. "Challenge accepted. I'll make a checklist of the rooms as soon as we're finished and keep track."

The dragon's outlook on this whole tour has suddenly taken a detour. "Is it different positions in every room? What exactly are our parameters?"

Creed laughs. "We'll come back to that. Carrying on. There's more to see."

CHAPTER NINETEEN

Rhylan

reed forces us to give up the conversation on christening the king's quarters but honestly, it's the most interesting part of this tour. That could also be because I've seen most of these rooms at one time or another.

Laryssa was paranoid when it came to security sweeps in her private quarters. Vik and I spent a great deal of our time scanning for listening devices and cameras in the two years we were in her service.

Ironic: Even knowing that, it was her planting listening devices that exposed me as a sympathizer.

Crazy how life turns out.

I tag along as Creed points out the kitchen, the informal sitting room, the nanny suite, and nursery—

"I had nothing to do with these rooms and have no plans on using them for years to come," Creed says, holding up his hand. "You are young and deserve to explore your wild side before needing to worry about procreating."

"Agreed," Keyla says looking around to all of us to make sure we're on the same page.

We all nod feverishly. It seems we all agree on that. No kids anytime soon. Thank the gods.

Creed's about to strike off into another round of door opening when I grab his arm. "As exciting as this all isn't—any chance we're going to start touring bedrooms? I've got to vet fifteen new security personnel, and someone mentioned a happy ending to this tour."

Creed looks to Keyla and Doc. "Where are you two on the tour?"

Keyla, bless her, takes one for the team. "I'm super excited to explore every inch of the suite, and I love that you're so excited about sharing it with us, but yes, I'd love to cut to the naked part. I too have a surprise that I'm eager to share with you... and it happens to be hidden under my skirt."

Creed barks a laugh and gestures down the hall. "Follow me."

When he strikes off toward the master suite, Keyla glances back at Doc and me and waggles her brow.

We grin like the lovesick fools we are and pick up the pace.

"Welcome to our suite," Creed says, pushing the doors open wide. "It took the staff almost four days to wipe every trace of Laryssa from this apartment and most importantly, from this suite. Everything here has been repainted, replaced, and restored to my specifications."

"It's wonderful," Keyla says, rushing over to the bed. "I'm guessing the bed is part of the replaced items. Your parents didn't sleep on a football field, did they?"

Creed laughs. "No. They had a normal, king-sized bed, but we are four to a bed. It's been a little snug in my bed the past few nights."

Dillan grins. "I don't know. I kinda like snug."

"Make no mistake. I do too. However, this gives us the option to not have to be snug if we want to spread out."

"It's perfect," Keyla says, unbuttoning the buttons of her blouse. "Well done. I can't wait—"

Creed shakes his head. "Oh, you need to wait, Little Wolf. Only a little longer."

"Seriously? You're killing me, Creed."

He barks a laugh. "Come. I swear you'll love this."

Keyla lets off a growl and her sexual frustration is too funny. Like Jaxx says, It's easier lettin' the cat outta the bag than it is stuffin' the thing back in.

Keyla's had a taste of what we can be, and our little wolf is hungry.

Creed takes a key out of his pocket and unlocks a door on the rounded wall on the far side of the room. "My father always kept the north turret of the tower as his observatory, but I moved his stargazing equipment into the sunroom and opted to remodel. Tell me if I got it right, Little Wolf. Is it everything you fantasized about?"

Keyla joins him in the doorway and looks inside. The squeal that bubbles out of her is the purest delight I've ever heard.

Curiosity peaked, I hustle to see what Creed did.

Keyla

It's a playroom. My very own kinky minx playroom to share with my mates. I take in the oddly shaped furniture and the feathers and straps and massage oils. I squee when I see the black leather sex shorts with silver buckles across the front. "Oh, like the ones in the catalog I wanted."

Creed chuckles. "I got a pair for each of us and picked up a few things for you too. You never mentioned what you'd like to be wearing in your kinky minx fantasies, so I took liberties and made a few selections."

Doc unhooks a hanger from the rack and lifts a red leather strappy outfit with strategically placed openings. His bear lets off a long rumble of appreciation. "Fuck yeah, you did. Nicely done, mate."

Rhylan's taking a walking tour, his eyes alight. Man, it's so different seeing his eyes and being able to read his emotions. I can't get over how much he takes my breath away.

"So now is it time for a happy ending?" I ask.

Creed nods. "Yes, Little Wolf. Where would you like to begin?"

I look around the room and smile. Kotah would be mortified if he knew I knew what he and Hawk ordered for their play-room, but I wasn't interested in most of it. I'm not looking for a lifestyle like Hawk enjoys, I just wanted some playtime toys.

Biting my bottom lip, I look around. Decisions. Decisions. I'll start with the outfit. Striding over to Doc, I take the hanger and head behind the little dressing screen.

How sexy.

"You boys can get naked or try on your sexy shorts, that's up to you. I'm giving this outfit a test run."

Behind the screen, I make quick work of my clothes and then take the leather strappy thing off the hanger. It's not the easiest thing to figure out, but I've always loved a good puzzle. Once I get my legs through the right holes and pull the shoulder straps in place, I adjust the bindings on my boobs and pull my boots back on.

Oh, they're going to love the boots.

Once they're on and zipped up, I unbraid my hair and rake it loose with my fingers. Primping up my boobs, I check myself in the mirror and then make sure everything that's supposed to be contained is contained and everything that's supposed to be exposed is exposed.

"You boys ready?"

"Yeah, babe," Dillan says, his voice husky. "Ready and waiting."

My heart is racing as I round the screen and find my three guys sporting sexy man shorts. I can't help the whimper that escapes my throat.

They are— "Oh gawd. Can I just say... the problem with crotchless outfits is that I just creamed the inside of my legs. You guys are so sinfully delicious."

Dillan chuckles, glancing down at the bulge pushing at the buckles straining to hold the front of his shorts. "I don't see the crotchless part of your outfit as a problem. The buckled front of ours might be though."

They are amazing.

"Rhy, grab your datapad and set it to take a picture of us. We're way too hot not to."

Creed chuckles. "Do you think that's a good idea? We're the King and Queen of Dornte. Our private selves can never collide with our public selves."

Rhylan grins. "Then it's a good thing I'm also a head of security. I'll take my datapad off the network and ensure the pictures are data-locked to this room. I'll cast them to that screen to show for us but no one else."

"Can you password protect them?" Doc asks.

"Can I fuck all night?"

"Hells yes, you can." I pump my fist in the air and stride, long-legged over to them in my kick-ass boots. "Gather round, boys. Your queen wants to play sexy photoshoot."

The four of us get handsy and naughty posing for pictures. It's hard to know where one of us ends and the others begin. It's also so much fun, I can't believe it.

At first, we're standing up and groping one another, boobs, bulges, and backsides. When Rhylan bends me over and runs his fingers through the opening of the crotchless outfit the dynamic changes.

"Sit here, Little Wolf."

I look down at the low to the ground, black leather chair and wonder about the missing section of the seat. It's a sleek design with a slanted back and nothing beneath the seat.

"It's a queening chair," Creed says. "I asked Hawk about some props for light play, and he stands behind these selections."

Doc chuckles. "He would know. From what Brant said, he was into some hard-core shit before their mating. He's toned it down now that he's committed, but they still call their private space the Den of Debauchery."

I wave that away and smile. "I'm happy with ours being a playroom, thanks. And the less we think about my brothers-in-law like that, the better."

"Agreed," Creed says.

Rhylan brings my attention back to the slimline, black leather chair. "Since you are our queen, this is your throne. Sit down and open your legs for us."

Unsure how it works, I sit, open my legs, and... yep, it quickly becomes clear.

Dillan drops to the floor on his back and slides under the seat. He seems a little too familiar with how this works, but I try not to think about that.

I am the one benefitting from all the experiences they had before. I win in the end.

His mouth latches onto my core and I arch into his kiss. "Sexy crotchless outfits are my new favorite thing."

Creed grins. "I'm glad you think so because there are more orders yet to arrive."

"Perfect."

Rhylan is watching us, loosening the buckles on the front of his shorts. "Is your photo bug satisfied or would you like some private pictures of this?"

I sit forward, my breath quickening as Dillan's soft stubble brushes my clit as his tongue flicks at my entrance. "No. No pictures like this... I'd like to play with your piercing though."

Rhylan grins. "Which one?"

I take inventory of his body accessories. He's got one piercing over his left brow, both his nipples have hoops, and then there's the one I'm talking about. "The one hiding under those leathers. Unbuckle and let loose... both of you."

"Yes, my queen." Rhylan makes quick work of the silver buckles of his sexy man shorts and springs his cock free. He doesn't take the shorts off, just opens the front and starts palming his erection.

Creed's ready at the same time. "Where do you want us, Little Wolf?"

I hold out both my hands. "Let me play while the two of you make out over me. I'm going to watch and enjoy the view."

Rhylan's dragon growls and he steps in close to my right. Creed moves to the left of my chair and then they lean in and start kissing.

I. Love. This. Chair.

The leather creaks as I shift my feet backward and twist to take Rhylan into my mouth. His hips sway, rocking the solid shaft of his cock in and out of my mouth.

On a retreat, I score the tender sheath of flesh with my teeth and then play with the piercing. Rolling the metal ball against my tongue, I push into the tiny slit and lick and suckle the drops of precum rising to the surface.

"You taste good, Dragon. Your queen is thirsty for more cum on my tongue."

Rhylan breaks from the hot and heavy kissing with Creed and sears me with a look. "If you keep this up, you're going to get a mouthful."

"Mmm."

Creed's cock pulses in my palm.

"You like that thought, my love?"

"The thought of Rhy shooting warm streams of cum against your tongue and down your throat? Yeah. It's fucking hot."

Dillan's growl vibrates against my core and a rush of cream meets his mouth. He's pushing, face-first into my crotch with a roughness he doesn't usually set free.

I'm pinned against his mouth and chin, his muscled arms hooked from under the chair and over my thighs. He flicks the entrance of my pussy with aggressive prodding, his grinding mouth rubbing my aching clit.

I gasp, riding his mouth, and go back to sucking Rhylan's cock.

"Fuck, yes," Creed says, his voice rough. "Eat her, Bear. She's close."

I suck to the end of Rhylan's cock and pop off. Shifting to the other hand, I swallow Creed down next.

"That's my girl," Creed says, gripping the back of my hair. "Fuck that's good, Little Wolf."

I'm bucking against the pressure of Dillan's mouth when his fingers slick through the hot mess and take over. Two fingers push inside me while his thumb moves back toward my ass. The depth of those probing digits is so good... especially with the teasing of his thumb.

"Suck Rhy," Creed says, pulling his hips back. "Our dragon wants to quench your thirst. Don't you, Rhy?"

"I do. Slecking hell, it won't take long."

I switch back to Rhylan's cock, losing my mind. My insides are pulsing around Dillan's fingers, gripping him in greedy squeezes that feel so good.

Rhylan groans above me and I glance up their bodies to see Creed kissing him with heated passion. Seeing the two of them in a lip-lock like that makes my wolf howl inside. They are so beautiful together.

Wanting all their sensations, I access our mental energies the way Creed always does and open us up. The bombardment of sensations is incredible.

The scents. The passions. The pleasures of the flesh.

Rhylan's hips lock and the hot streams of his release coat my tongue. I swallow and suck, my wolf growling for more. He obliges.

Wave after wave of salty cream fills my mouth and I swallow him down. So good. He's in ecstasy and I feel how deeply this connection touches him.

Lost in the shared eroticism, there's no way I can hold off. I come hard against Dillan's mouth, my wolf howling at the perfection of it all.

Deep voices growl something I miss entirely and then the world spins around me. The next thing I know, my knees are on the padded mat, and I'm being penetrated from behind with my bear growling.

The keening grip of my orgasm takes another crazy run at me as Dillan slams deep inside me. I press my palms against the padded flooring, bracing myself as I come apart again.

"Oh, yes," I groan, arching against his thrusts. "I love you rough, Bear."

His thumb is still playing, probing the tight flesh of my ass. After my orgasm dies down, he withdraws and swipes the moisture from our joining to slick me there. "I need to fuck you, babe. I know you haven't had anything more than finger play, but my bear needs to mark you."

I wriggle my butt in invitation.

"Here," Creed says, rushing in with a bottle of clear liquid. "Prime her well or it'll burn."

Dillan prods and plays, slicking me with moisture until he squares his hips and presses inside. I swallow and try to catch my breath. My bear's cock is much bigger than their fingers. It's invasive and strange, but I've seen how much the boys like it and give it a moment.

"You good, babe?"

"I am. Yeah." As a wolf wildling, I've seen pack members like this during ritual nights and seasonal runs. I've always wondered what it would be like.

Now, I'm about to find out.

"Start slow. You're really big."

He chuckles. "You're so sweet."

"Anal takes getting used to," Creed says, lying down on the floor beside me. He shifts to take my breast into his mouth and then pinches my nipple with his teeth. "But if you like it, it'll open up many more opportunities for the four of us to share."

Rhylan lays on the floor on the other side of me and does the same thing, taking the other breast into his mouth before easing back to grin up at me. "And if you don't like it, that's fine too. That leaves more ass play for the rest of us."

He winks and I chuckle. Relaxing helps.

The burn is easing off, morphing toward pleasure.

"I feel so full."

Creed chuckles, reaching down my abdomen and brushing his fingers over my clit. "Wait until we fuck your pussy at the same time. Then you'll be doubly full."

"Mhmm... I like that idea." I swallow, grinding gently up and down Dillan's erection, getting a feel of what anal is like. "Why don't one of you shift under me and we'll do that now."

Creed laughs. "So eager. You're tight, Little Wolf. Give your body a chance to adjust. We'll get there. We have a lifetime to claim everything this mating offers."

Dillan gasps behind me, his fingers gripping into my hips as I ride his cock at my own pace. "You're torturing me, babe. Slow is heaven... but it's also torture."

Hearing the breathless desperation in Dillan's voice is incredibly sexy. I close my eyes and stop thinking about what we're doing and get back to feeling it. "Creed, finger me and play with my clit while Doc fucks my ass."

"Yes ma'am," Creed says.

"I love your dirty mouth," Rhylan says, shifting his attention back to my nipples.

I close my eyes and focus. My clit is swollen and sensitive from Dillan's play earlier. Even the first brush of Creed's fingers brings my next orgasm rising forward.

Dillan is moving now, his easy strokes filling me as my next release builds deep in my belly. I swallow and take it all in. The playful teasing. The dedication. The loving connections forming between the four of us.

I love my life.

"More." That one word escapes my throat with barely more than a whisper, but they hear me. And they give me what I ask for.

More stroking. More sucking. More thrusting.

Arms flexed tight, I grip the mat with white knuckles. I push back each time Dillan's pelvis hits my ass and the *slap-slap-slap* of each thrust is getting louder and faster. Creed's fingers penetrate, stroking against the ache of my clit. Rhylan plays with my breasts, nipping and sucking one while tweaking the nipple of the other.

It's *sooo* good.

The orgasm swirling inside me like a violent storm shatters and explodes. It steals my control and leaves me in a state of raw, carnal pleasure.

The scent of our sweat and sex. The sounds we make… I am destroyed and at the same time, more alive than I've ever been.

I tilt my head back and my wolf howls.

Dillan lets off a throaty grunt behind me and the thrusting stops. My legs quiver under the strain of supporting my weight, my energy spent.

We collapse into a sweaty heap of tangled limbs and Dillan

spoons me from behind. I close my eyes and focus on getting reacquainted with oxygen. His heart is hammering against my back, and it takes us both a long while before our breathing returns to normal.

CHAPTER TWENTY

Keyla

Having just gone through the coronation process for Kotah a month ago, with Isabo's help, I am in fine form for overseeing the preparations for Creed's celebration. He's perfectly capable of doing it himself, but why should he have to plan his own party? He should be able to sit back and enjoy it.

"Welcome all, to the pre-drink event," I say, opening the door for my brother and his mates. "Creed's so happy you could join us."

"We wouldn't miss it," Kotah says, hugging me.

"Still, it's a lot of travel for you guys going back and forth a couple of times a week."

"We don't mind," Calli says. "Hawk is used to gallivanting across the country and with his private jet, and if it brings us to you and Honor, we'll deal."

"Meh," Brant waggles his brows. "It's perfectly enjoyable when you use the time wisely."

I laugh and point at him. "Don't elaborate."

Kotah chuckles. "Ignore him. The travel time is fine and soon it'll be even better. We've been working on our plans for the Pennsylvania Prime Palace and things are shaping up."

I'm so excited about that.

"Is Lukas here?" Hawk asks.

"No, he moved into our room of the heir's suite and is keeping an eye on her tonight. Shadow's been sitting with her and he thinks there has been some progress with her cognitive awareness."

Calli grins. "That's fantastic. I can't wait to check in on her."

I nod. "You guys can either claim a guest room in our suite here or claim the Auburn Suite and be close to Honor and Lukas, whichever you prefer."

Kotah waves that away. "I want to be with you, to see where you're living, and spend time with your mates in your new home."

I'm glad. I want that too.

"Then I suppose I should invite you past the front foyer then, shouldn't I? We'll save the grand tour for after the coronation. For now, Rhy and Doc are waiting in the great room. We figured we'd have a drink and you all can relax and watch things on the wall screen while we're gone."

"So, like the green room before the big television debut?" Jaxx asks, following my lead.

"More like watching the game at the pub," I say, rounding the corner of the wall into the great room. "And you're playing the part of the bartender, Jaxx. I think you should have everything you need."

Jaxx stalls out, wide-eyed, and whistles a catcall. "Oh, prepare to get roostered, all of ya."

Calli laughs. "Lasso it in, cowboy. We're not here to get roostered. We're having a celebration drink before Creed and Keyla go on a quadrant-wide broadcast. Them falling over drunk is not the goal here."

Doc raises his tumbler as the quint come in and settle. "The moment Keyla and I saw this room, we thought of you, Jaguar."

Jaxx's long-legged strides carry him across the polished stone floor and around the couches. Once behind the bar, he starts taking inventory of what he has to work with. "Is it my birthday? It feels like it."

While he's acting foolish and entertaining everyone, I jog upstairs to check on the man of the hour. When I don't find him in our suite, I keep searching until I end up in our shared office.

"Hey. Is everything all right? The quint's here and we're getting ready for your coronation toast."

He looks up from behind his desk and pushes a wooden box toward me. "Sorry. I got lost in thought."

I read his intention for me to open it and take a look. It's a signet ring with the Thornebane crest on it. "Is this your father's?"

He shakes his head. "A replacement. Laryssa had the original melted down and destroyed. It's the same though. It's the symbolism that counts, I suppose."

I pick it up and sit on his desk facing him. "So, is there a reason you're sitting in here staring at a replica of your father's ring while we have family downstairs and a quadrant waiting to watch you claim your crown?"

He looks up at me and shrugs. "I always thought I'd look forward to ruling. I planned for it my whole life. I hungered for it over the past two years. Now that it's here, I'd give anything for my father to be alive a little longer. He was a great king. What if I don't measure up? What if I get it all wrong?"

I pluck the ring out of its padded housing and claim his hand. "I bet, when your father was facing his coronation, he spoke those same words to your mother. Being a great ruler doesn't come from having all the answers, it comes from being willing to admit you don't have all the answers and surrounding your-self with capable people who you can trust."

I slide the ring onto his finger and then hike my skirt so I can widen my legs to straddle his lap. Reaching around his neck to the back, I kiss the worry lines on his forehead. "You and I are here for our citizens. We want the best for them. We'll heal this quadrant together and we'll learn to be great leaders together."

He leans forward and kisses the royal banding on my throat. "I appreciate what you're saying—and you're right—but if we don't get up and leave right now, I'll need to fuck you on this desk. Sadly, even leaving right now, I may have a noticeable hard-on during my coronation telecast."

I burst out laughing and hop up. "Not what I was going for, sorry."

"Not your fault. It seems I can't be anywhere near you before my need for you burns hot in my blood."

I let my wolf rise to the surface and growl for him. "That goes both ways."

I kiss him and now I'm the one with sexual need zinging in my blood. I swallow and pull him out of the office and toward the stairs. "We need to surround ourselves with other people."

He chuckles. "Good idea."

The two of us walk hand-in-hand toward the stairs. Everything is still so new, but I hardly remember my life before Creed looked into my eyes that first time.

"I'm sorry Honor couldn't stand with you today."

He shrugs. "Me too. It has only been a week. I have faith Lukas will break the Blood Witch's curses. And with my efforts trying to reach her with mind energy, I have faith she'll wake up soon."

"Me too."

We round the post to the stairs and start to descend together. "And when she does, we'll all be together to ensure she lives a long and happy life. She deserves it."

"She does—"

Creed's expression pinches a moment before he winces and doubles over. "Fuck, that hurts."

I grab hold of him, worried that he might fall down the stairs. "What is it? What's wrong?"

A scream bursts from his lips as he curls in on himself, panting. I barely catch him but there's a real chance both of us will topple down the stairs.

"Help!"

The powerful flap of wings brings the arrival of Hawk's wildling form almost immediately after I call out. He transforms back into a man in time to block us from tumbling down the steps.

Doc is there a couple of seconds later and then everyone is helping and grabbing and carrying Creed down to the floor on the main level of our suite.

"What's wrong?" Doc asks, dropping to the ground beside him. "Where's the pain?"

Creed

"My back. Worse than it's ever been. It's on fire. Fuck, make it stop." The pain is sharp and floods my body. The cursed beast within me roars as red-hot agony burns through my cells.

"How attached are you to this shirt?"

"Fuck the shirt."

"Jaxx, get it off him."

I close my eyes, gasping as Jaxx slices down my back. The rending of fabric signals the end of that shirt's usefulness.

"What's happening?" Keyla asks.

"What the fuck are we looking at?" Jaxx asks.

There's a round of male cursing and then someone grabs my

ankle. By the rush of soothing energy, it must be Kotah. "All will be well, brother-mine. We are here for you."

"Why is his back doing that?" Brant asks.

"I think it's his wings," Doc says. "Part of his torture was having them shorn off. Do wings grow back?"

"We used my tears on him a week or two ago. Could that have started the process?" Calli asks.

"Or the curse is weakening?" Hawk suggests.

"What do we do?" Keyla asks.

"It looks like they're trying to break out," Dillan says. "I say we make two surgical cuts and see what happens. Creed? Any objections to that?"

"I don't give a fuck. Just do something."

"Okay, someone go and grab my medical bag from the foyer closet."

Keyla lays down facing me and clutches my hand and Rhylan spoons her so they're both there. "We've got you, my prince. We're here."

"All right," Dillan says. "This might hurt but with the amount of pain you're already in, I doubt it."

I feel the pressure of the blade pressing against the flesh of my back but he's right, it doesn't hurt. In a sea of pain, it's a small ripple on the surface.

"Almost there," Doc says. "It *is* your wings. They regrew and are trapped. Once they're free, this will all be over. It's like a monarch trying to burst out of a cocoon."

"Hang in there." Rhylan's gaze is bright and beautiful. Fuck I love seeing his eyes.

Bone snaps inside me and the crack ricochets inside my skull. I twist, screaming as blood runs hot down my sides. "Fuck. Get them free."

I can't focus. I release Keyla's hand for fear of breaking it. Rolling onto my stomach, I press my forehead against the polished marble of the floor.

My back is on fire, my skin aflame. Bones and cartilage snap and reform, as my wings break through. The pain is cosmic. It obliterates all thought, all sound.

And then... it stops.

~

Doc

When Creed falls still, I'm not sure if he blacked out, dropped dead, or what. The dropped dead worry is answered quickly because his chest is still heaving with the pain and his entire body is shaking.

"Is it over?" Keyla blinks up at me with tears pooling in her eyes.

"Yeah, I think so."

"Fucking hell," Hawk says, stepping back to sit on the steps. "That was intense, Creed. Glad it's over."

Creed barks a laugh that holds no humor and falls limp against the floor. "Yeah, me too."

"How about we give the four of you a moment of privacy," Calli says.

"Yeah," Jaxx says. "We'll be in the great room drinkin' hard and trying to numb the past five minutes from our minds."

"Save us one," I hand Brant my scalpel and point toward the kitchen. "Just leave it on the counter. I'll take care of cleaning it later."

When it's just the four of us, I drop to one knee to check on our mate. "How are you doing?"

"I've been better." Creed's voice is a little raw, but his gaze is focused and his breathing is normalizing.

I take the discarded tatters of his shirt and wipe up some of the blood on his sides and down his ribs. "I hate to be the one to bring it up, but we need to get you upstairs. You need a quick shower and a fresh outfit before your coronation broadcast, and we've got no time."

"Fuck."

"Yeah, that pretty much covers it."

"Can't a guy wallow in his agony for five minutes?"

Rhylan chuckles. "Not if that guy is about to be made king of the quadrant."

Creed groans and moves to push up onto his palms. He's got nothing left and gets nowhere.

"Need a little help, mate?" I grip under his arm on one side while Rhylan grabs the other.

Together, we get him back up to our bedroom and into the ensuite. "This isn't as sexy as our usual strip you down, but it'll have to do. You know, with the entire quadrant waiting on you and all."

Keyla is already beautiful in her queenly gown, so Rhylan and I strip down and help him in.

"Don't get his hair wet if you don't have to," she says. "We don't have time for it to dry again."

I sweep the length of his silver mane up and hold it out of the way from the spray.

"How do they look?" Creed asks, still barely strong enough to lift his head. "Are they fully restored?"

"Are they supposed to be black and turquoise with sparkles catching the light?" I ask.

His entire body seems to relax with his exhale. "Yes. Thank the gods."

Rhylan and I get the blood rinsed away and turn off the water as quickly as we can. Keyla meets us with a towel. "I've got another outfit set out on the bed. How does dressing work with wings?"

Creed seems to be rousing a bit and starts supporting his weight. "Faeries usually withdraw their wings, wear clothing designed to go around the wing blades, go shirtless, or wear a vest."

"I looked around your closet and didn't see anything but dress shirts."

"That's because I didn't have wings when I packed to move into this suite."

"We don't have time to go back to the heirs' suite and get something."

Creed straightens and stands on his own for the first time, glancing in the mirror. "No, we don't, but I think my father's battle leathers are in the chest in the office. I asked Isabo to put them there for me."

Rhylan jogs off and returns a few minutes later with a set of spank brown and silver leathers. He pulls the pants on commando, which is sexy as fuck, and then Rhy helps him on with the battle vest.

Keyla steps behind him and straightens his long silver hair between his wings.

The king is ready to represent.

"Damn, Creed," I say, grinning. "You fucking rock those leathers. All I'm picturing now is the coronation afterparty."

Rhy jogs out of the bathroom, tucking his shirt back in, once again ready for the coronation. "I'm with our bear. We need to have another sexy playroom photoshoot with you wearing that."

Keyla chuckles. "Doc likes that idea too much. Dude, settle that bad boy down. We'll be in front of our citizens in less than five minutes."

The three of them all shift their gazes to my cock, and it stands up strong and proud. "Staring at him isn't helping. But yeah, I'll get dressed."

Creed grins. "Let's get this done and get back here quickly. The king wants private time with his mates."

I grab my clothes and put a little hustle into it.

Yeah, life is good.

CHAPTER TWENTY-ONE

Creed

The next few days pass with an unusual calmness. After the past two years, it keeps me off balance to have things going so smoothly. Keyla and I spend a great deal of time together in the study laying out our plans for the quadrant. As different as our realms might be, we see things in much the same light. Collaboration with her is an incredible addition to my confidence in leading.

And it's not only my relationship with Keyla that is working out better than I ever thought possible.

After spending our days with the citizens of the Dornte, Keyla and I come back to the King's Tower and spend our evenings with our mates, laughing, fucking, and generally enjoying one another's company.

It's the happiest I've ever been.

The only dark spot is Honor's inability to share it with me.

"What time are you expecting them to come through?" Rhy asks, checking his watch.

Even standing beneath the shaded overhang of the Dornte

Portal Hub's pick-up area, Rhylan's eyes practically glow in the light. It's incredible to see him show himself to the world. He's not only good-looking, but with his hair out of his face, his personality shines through for all the world to see.

Keyla shrugs, waving to someone in the crowd, and smiles like she's seen a dear friend. "Not sure. The time between the other realm and this one is wonky. I never know if it's day or night back home. I'm sure they'll be here soon."

I follow her delighted gaze and recognize the green-skinned, wrinkle-faced trylle and pixie woman with ombre blue hair and fluttering silver wings.

"Who's that?" Rhy asks.

"It's two of the faery outcasts and unwanteds—the people in the underground tunnels who gave us shelter beneath the city that first night we needed refuge during the hours of curfew."

"You mean the hours while Doc and I scoured the city searching for you and cleaning up the mess you left behind when you killed Riven."

Huh, I never thought much about that once we got out of there. "Yeah, then. Thanks for that. Is there anything I should be worried about on that front let me know before it bites me in the ass."

Rhylan frowns. "Why would it bite you?"

"Because I killed a man and fled the scene."

Rhy rolls his eyes. "And you're just getting around to worrying about that now?"

I grin. "It's been a busy couple of weeks."

"Yeah, it has." Rhylan chuckles and waves my concern away. "I took care of it. You're fine."

"Creed, come over and say hello," Keyla says, waving me over to join her. "You remember Coal and Lyree from the tunnels."

I leave Rhy and Dillan at the shuttle van and join her. I don't think I knew the woman's name, but I remember her. "Yes, of course. How are you both?"

The two seem flustered but Keyla hugs them like they are family, and they seem to relax. "We are well, thank you, Majesty," Lyree says. "Congratulations on reclaiming the realm. We are all so pleased for you."

"You played an important part in that," Keyla says. "You helped two strangers in a dangerous time. That says a lot about you. We will always be grateful."

Coal clears his throat. "The universe simply placed the people you needed in your path. All is as it was meant to be."

"Beautifully said," Keyla says. "And now that the obstacles have been removed, Dornte is well on its way to being restored as a quadrant of peace and honor."

Coal smiles at her and I see the affection in his dark, black eyes. I can hardly fault the male for being enamored. I think everyone who meets Keyla is a little thunderstruck... but perhaps I'm biased.

~

Rhylan

Doc and I watch Keyla and Creed interacting with a couple of citizens in the crowd and I smile. The two of them in action is living magic at work. Soul-seared is a crazy concept but anyone seeing the two of them together can see they are a perfect match.

"Taking in the sights?" Dillan asks, leaning against the side of the van.

"Sometimes they steal my breath. Well, honestly, there are moments it all steals my breath."

The bear grunts and nods. "Same. There are moments one of you will say something or do something and I feel like it's all too perfect—like the hammer is about to drop or the alarm will go off and I'll wake up and it'll all disappear like a fading dream."

"Do you think it's because everything sucked so badly before them and we're afraid to go back to that?"

"Maybe. My life didn't suck but it certainly didn't live up to this."

"Do you miss being a doctor?"

He shrugs. "I had patients in a small town, local clinic with two other family practitioners. My patients will still get the care they need, and I've done enough patching up of our own family to keep me busy... for now anyway. Maybe when things settle down, I'll look into private care here. Not sure."

I sigh. "Part of me is afraid to lay roots. I worry I'm going to sleck it up and lose it all."

Dillan lays a heavy arm across my shoulder and tilts his head to touch mine. "Then we make a pact. I won't let you fuck it up if you do the same for me. Us aggressive, mouthy, hot-heads need to stick together."

I laugh. "Sounds good."

The two of us fall quiet for a moment and I'm back to watching Creed and Keyla. "It's good to see them so much in love. The realm deserves an amazing couple at the helm."

He nods. "It does... and they certainly are that. We're pretty fucking lucky."

"You don't need to tell me."

Dillan squeezes my shoulder and I meet his gaze. "Are you doing all right, Dragon? You haven't talked about Vikarus, and you don't have to if you're not ready, but I thought I should check. What went down with him and your mom... it was cold. It must've left deep cuts."

"Oh, it did. I'm all kinds of messed up about it. I'm hurt and angry and a million other things but honestly, I don't care. I've twisted myself in knots for years to make things right for my family and they hung me out to dry. I'm glad it worked out for them, but I'm out. You three are my life now."

Doc nods. "Good call. We've got your back."

~

Keyla

"They're here, babe."

I acknowledge Dillan's update, see the quint coming through the main entrance of the portal hub, and then return my attention to our tunnel friends. "We have to run, but don't be strangers. You are not unwanteds anymore. If there is ever anything we can do to help make life in Dornte better, please come to the castle and speak to us."

"Yes, Milady," Coal says.

I wink. "My friends call me Keyla, and you two most definitely fall into that category."

The pixie, Lyree blushes and bows her head. "It was lovely to see you both again. Blessed be."

"Blessed be," Creed says, easing me back and redirecting us toward the crowd gathered at the shuttle bus. "Lukas, it's good to have you back. Did you have any luck?"

He tilts his head from side to side, considering. "Some. I've cleared out her condo and everything I found interesting and worth a closer look, I boxed to bring to the castle." He points to three large boxes stacked on a rolling cart. "There's enough here to keep me busy for a long while."

"Well, any help you can offer, is greatly appreciated. I had hoped that once the witch was dead, her curse would wane, and Honor would wake."

He shakes his head. "I would've been surprised if that's how it worked. Not to worry. I'll set up in the suite and continue to work on unraveling things. It's not time to panic yet."

Too late. Creed's putting up a brave front, but I know he's panicked that him killing the Blood Witch against Lukas's advisement cost Honor her chance at recovery.

"I'm so grateful you've agreed to stay with us and try to help

Honor," I say, hugging Lukas. He stiffens at the contact and Calli chuckles at me as they approach. The two of us have been trying to wear Lukas down a little and get him conditioned to life with us.

Hugging is a big part of that.

I leave Creed to speak with Lukas and join Dillan as he closes the distance to greet Kotah and the quint.

My brother sweeps me up in a bone-crushing hug and kisses my temple. "I've missed you, little one."

I chuckle. "I'm the queen of a quadrant now. I don't think I'm your little one any longer."

He scoffs and presses his forehead to mine. "You will always be my little sister." Breathing deep, he makes no secret that he's assessing my scent. "And the mating has been going well, I see. All four of your scents have merged quite completely. Come. I want you to tell me all about it."

I chuckle. "Seriously? You want to know the details of how my sex life with my three mates is going?"

He laughs and eases back. "Not at all. A simple yes or no on the mating information and then details of your new life unfolding."

"Then yes, everything is going very well—very, very well, actually."

Calli grins. "Ignore him. I want you to dish all the nitty-gritty details."

Kotah tenses and makes a face.

I take pity on him. "Later, when we're alone."

"Awesome." Calli hugs me next and then points to the shuttle van. "Is this us?"

"Yeah."

"Great. I'm going to grab a seat. I'm pooped."

"I'll sit with you, *Chigua*," Kotah says. "Come, let's get you off your feet." I chuckle as my brother sweeps under Calli's knees and carries her onto the bus.

"When he says he wants her off her feet, he's quite literal," Shadow says, smiling.

I smile at the elf, thankful that he made the trip to join us. "The four of them are so obsessively attentive over Calli and the baby it's crazy. Little Liza will be spoiled before she's even born."

"That's lovely, actually."

"It is." I eye up the suitcase beside his foot and take Shadow's hands in mine. "Thank you for coming. I know this is a temporary thing while you explore what this realm has to offer you, but I hope you love it. I know you can do great things to help us heal the lives of the people of Dornte."

"I look forward to making a difference." When a gust of a breeze catches his dark purple hair, he captures the errant strands and tucks them behind his long, pointed ears. "So, this is StoneHaven."

"Part of it," I say, "but the people of this realm have divided things differently over time. This is Dornte, one of four quadrants of the realm and in the center is the historical city of StoneHaven."

"Much to learn, then," he says.

"For us all."

"Are we set?" Hawk asks, checking that we're all here. "We've got a hungry bear and a female that's dying to see her bestie."

I giggle. "Then why are we hanging out at the portal station? Let's go home."

The whole gang climbs into the shuttle and everyone takes their seats.

"Did you mean what you said just now, Little Wolf?" Creed asks. "Do you consider the castle home?"

I think about that, and the reality warms my insides. "Yes, I do. It's where we belong, where we're needed, but more than that, it's where the four of us fell in love. If home is where the heart is, then Thornebane Castle is definitely our home."

~~ THE END ~~

Thank you for reading Dark Crown the eighth book in the Guardians of the Fae Realms series and the final book of Keyla's harem – The Darkness Trilogy.
If you are inclined to help a girl out, it would be amazing if you could leave a star rating or review for Dark Crown. It tells me what you thought about the story, and helps other readers find books they might like.
Claim book 9 – Honor Restored and find out what happens next in the lives of the Guardians of the Fae Realms.

HONOR RESTORED:

The reign of the usurper queen is over...

Since before the time of the Wars of Power, Thornebane siblings have ruled Dornte—the male as Guardian of the Quadrant and the female as the Guardian of the Crown.

Two years after my parents were murdered and their crown stolen, my brother reclaims leadership of the Dornte quadrant and rescues me from the pri son she cursed me into.

My mentor is dead, my training incomplete, and my recent trauma more than I can deal with alone.

Thankfully, I'm not alone.

Claim your copy now: Honor Restored

Author Notes

Written on 06/9/2021

Thank you for reading Dark Crown and since you're reading this, for sticking with me... lol.

I have three more trilogies planned for this series and am looking forward to writing the stories to come. Honor is next.

Like Rhylan said, *To cut off the head of the snake is not enough. Weeding out the evils rooted and woven into the fGuardians of the Phoenix.ecessary.*

Don't miss out on what happens next with Honor as she recovers and finds her footing with her mates.

I promise, it will be a fun and sexy ride.

Grab the first book in the trilogy here.

As always, if you want to check in with me, I welcome the chance to chat. I'm active on FB and pretty good at getting to my emails.

Hugs to all,

JL

Find Me

My Direct Sales Site: Shopify

My books

Web page – www.jlmadore.com
Email – jlmadorewrites@gmail.com
Newsletter – JL Series Updates

ALSO BY JL MADORE

JL's Reverse Harem Titles

Guardians of the Fae Realms

Guardians of the Phoenix – Calli's Harem

Book 1 – Rise of the Phoenix

Book 2 – Wolf's Soul

Book 3 – Bear's Strength

Book 4 – Hawk's Heart

Book 5 – Jaguar's Passion

Darkness Calls – Keyla's harem

Book 6 – Dark Curse

Book 7 – Dark Soul

Book 8 – Dark Crown

Guardians of the Crown – Honor's Harem

Book 9 – Honor Restored

Book 10 – Honor Guards

Book 11 – Honor Bound

Book 12 – Honor Empowered

Rise of the Amberloq – Lark's Harem

Book 13 – Find the Fallen

Book 14 – Rise from Ruin

Book 15 – Trust and Triumph

Exemplar Hall

Exemplar Hall – Jesse's Harem

Book 1 – Captured by the Magi

Book 2 – Jesse and the Magi Vault

Book 3 – The Makings of a Magi Knight

Book 4 – Clash with the Magi Council

Book 5 – The Unstoppable Storme

Club Sanguine

Book 1 – Moonstone Maelstrom

Book 2 - Sunstone Sacrifice

JL's More Traditional M/F, M/M, or Menage

The Watchers of the Gray Series (Paranormal)

Book 1 – Watcher Untethered – Zander

Book 2 – Watcher Redeemed – Kyrian

Book 3 – Watcher Reborn – Danel

Book 4 – Watcher Divided – Phoenix

Book 5 – Watcher United – Seth

Book 6 – Watcher Compelled – Bo

Book 7 – Watcher Unfeigned – Brennus

Book 8 – Watcher Exposed – Taharqa

The Scourge Survivor Series (Fantasy)

Book 1 – Blaze Ignites

Book 2 – Ursa Unearthed

Book 3 – Torrent of Tears

Book 4 – Blind Spirit

Book 5 – Fate's Journey

Book 6 – Savage Love – epilogue novella

Aliens of Atlantis Series (Sci-Fi)

Book 1 – Taryn's Tiderider

Book 2 – Kai's Captive

Book 3 – Alyandra's Shadow

www.ingramcontent.com/pod-product-compliance
Lightning Source LLC
Chambersburg PA
CBHW050423260626
47156CB00003B/1136